7/5/... —

To

It has been great working with you. I hope you enjoy this "yarn."

Jack Owen

MYSTERY in the HIGH CASCADES

MYSTERY in the HIGH CASCADES

Jack Owen

Northwest Publishing, Inc.
Salt Lake City, Utah

Mystery in the High Cascades

All rights reserved.
Copyright © 1995 Northwest Publishing, Inc.

Reproduction in any manner, in whole or in part,
in English or in other languages, or otherwise
without written permission of the publisher is prohibited.

This is a work of fiction.
All characters and events portrayed in this book are fictional,
and any resemblance to real people or incidents is purely coincidental.

For information address: Northwest Publishing, Inc.
6906 South 300 West, Salt Lake City, Utah 84047
JC 11-10-94
Edited by Robin Larsen

PRINTING HISTORY
First Printing 1995

ISBN: 1-56901-458-2

NPI books are published by Northwest Publishing, Incorporated,
6906 South 300 West, Salt Lake City, Utah 84047.
The name "NPI" and the "NPI" logo are trademarks belonging to
Northwest Publishing, Incorporated.

PRINTED IN THE UNITED STATES OF AMERICA.
10 9 8 7 6 5 4 3 2 1

Dedicated to Barbara,
my wife and love for forty years,
who encouraged me during the writing.

Acknowledgments

I want to thank Barbara for her hours of editing, and Mark and Anne for reading, and making suggestions, to Les for helping with the instructions on marketing, and all my friends who cared.

1

The intrusion into our lives that was to come from our little holiday was completely unexpected, and quite dangerous. The specter of death by murder, the concealment, and the aura of violence surrounding it, had no place in the peaceful central Oregon mountains with their deep blue lakes, and pine needle trails through the pristine forests of tall Douglas fir. The mystery that was to unfold in those remote mountain recesses would lead us back into the crime-ridden cities of Oregon, where the overburdened police were struggling to keep up with the street violence and crime. Murder was becoming nearly a nightly occurrence. And when murder touches its victim, it also stains those who innocently brush against it. But I am getting ahead of the story, so let me tell it as it unfolded with all its impact and surprises.

It was a beautiful sunny day in Portland, and I was restless. I was unemployed, and had been for three months. After thirty years in the manufacturing of sawmill equipment, I had been caught up in the legal battles between the conservationists and the timber industry. I loved the forests in Oregon, and I ached because of the damage caused by the methods and excesses in the harvesting of the timber in them. I also knew that I had earned a good living, raised my children, been a good citizen, lived what I felt was a Christian life, all due to the cutting down of the very trees I loved. And the terribly sad part was that there were thousands of other lives affected, who were closer to the battle front. They were affected by the indecision of the federal government, who had the power to regulate, but couldn't decide on how to do it.

The spotted owl was the flag that was being waved by the scientists that our old growth was being depleted. It was also a flag being waved by the timber industry to rally the troops to stave off the loss of a way of life that had existed for over a hundred years. The people caught in such a vise grip of inaction and frustration could only wait and see what their future would hold. Even the waiting itself was a method of self-destruction, because of the introspection process in job loss and resulting perceived loss of self-worth.

This was where I was coming from, and I wanted to get out and go. I was sitting in the backyard in a lawn chair watching the birds wash themselves in the birdbath, and I yelled into the house for Sara to come and see. I was pretty sure that she was being driven half crazy by my inability to concentrate for more than a few minutes on any single item. But she came out and nodding at the birds, said with a resigned smile on her face, "Is this what you wanted me to see, John?"

"Sure!" I said jokingly. "How would you like to take off to a mountain lake for a few days and splash in the water and soak up the sunshine?"

"Free as the birds?" she laughed.

"Right on!" I said expectantly.
"When? Tomorrow?" she asked.
"Sooner the better. I would like to get away for a while. Wouldn't you like to go camping and see some new country?"
"Sure!" she replied. "Give me some time to get everything together. You get the trailer out of the garage, and I'll see what we need to pack. We could probably leave in the morning."

After a day of preparation of food and packing, we were heading for the paradise of central Oregon, where the trails lead to the spectacular, the lakes are cold and refreshing, and the trees are so close that they seem to surround you like a warm blanket. Tall and majestic Douglas fir, ponderosa pine and smaller jack pine that have stood for hundreds of years welcomed thousands of visitors each year. We were ready for their hospitality and comfort.

We pulled out of our driveway at ten o'clock on Monday morning, July 9th, after making arrangements with our next-door neighbor to bring in the mail and papers. Our leaving with our trailer had over the years created somewhat of a stir in the neighborhood, because of our luck with the weather. It was in jest that they would get their lawn fertilizer out, because it was definitely going to rain. But with a smile, a friendly wave, and with their wishes of a good camping trip, we were off to God's country.

The tensions began to slip away as we traveled through the lush green Oregon valley nestled between the Cascade Mountain Range and the Pacific Coastal Range, and then through the forested Santiam Mountain Pass leading into the central Oregon communities. The Santiam Pass road followed the cascading North Santiam River that cut a deep gorge through the mountains wide enough to carry the spring runoff and supply a roadbed notched out of the mountainside. The little villages nestled along its banks were home to the fishermen, loggers and mill workers that had lived there for years. With the disappearance of the sawmills there were fewer people now, but the sturdy and the hopeful still stayed on. A more beautiful place to live was hard to find.

We could see the distant snow-covered peaks of Mt. Washington and Mt. Jefferson as we traveled on toward our home for a week that we had chosen near Paulina Lake, some thirty-four miles south of Bend. Passing through the tall red ponderosa pine stand of trees, the road seemed to be a royal carpet spreading out before us, leading up to a throne that was just over the next rise. And over the next rise was another carpet just like it. The carpet ran directly into the town of Sisters.

The town of Sisters is situated at the junction of Highway #20 to Bend and #126 to Redmond, and #242 over the McKenzie Pass. Sisters, with its false store fronts and old Western boardwalks, and a history that is quite fascinating, beckoned for us to stop. A short break for lunch was in order, so we chose the Wagon Wheel Restaurant. We were treated to a Western-type hamburger that was easily six inches across, and baked beans that were simply out of this world. Sara, choosing a somewhat smaller plate lunch, began making conversation about the decor that was not unique, but interesting, and so were some of the customers. She said of a short, wiry cowboy with boots, hat and all, "He certainly looks like he has just come in off the range. He fits in with the decor, doesn't he?"

Looking around at the paintings of cows grazing in front of the snow-covered peaks in the background, and cowboys lazing on their saddles, I nodded and said," His hat looks like it has seen better days, and so does he, but he sure looks like he belongs around here."

As he passed our booth to leave, I noticed his weathered face and the sweat darkened brim of his hat. A face that was weathered by the sun until brown as leather, but as sturdy and dependable as the West itself. We watched as he climbed into a large pickup truck that was pulling a double horse trailer with a sign on the door that identified the owner as "THE PAULINA LAKE LODGE." Inside the trailer were two horses that looked as if they had been well cared for, their coats shining in the sunlight as he pulled away. As I gazed after him, I said, "Wouldn't you like to hear some of his stories?"

Sara, knowing how old timers sometimes spin a yarn when they have tourists as an audience, mused, "Oh, I don't know! It gets pretty deep with you around, sometimes." Her dancing eyes told me she had a touch of the Old West herself! We paid up and left, heading southeast toward Bend.

The traffic was heavy through Bend, a bustling growing city which once was a stopping place for wagon trains. It was called Farewell Bend as the wagons continued onward north and west to The Dalles, and on to Portland. According to some historians, the Deschutes River, winding its way through the alpine meadows from its source near Little Lava Lake, became the stopping place for the wagon trains coming West. The town grew along its banks, but the name for the settlement was harder to settle upon than the river. At first they named it after the river, and the town became known as Deschutes. Later, it took on the name of Farewell Bend, because the travelers going on to The Dalles saw their last bend in the river as it plunged on westward through plains to join up with the Crooked and Metolious Rivers, and on into the Columbia River. The town was given its official name of Bend by the U.S. Postal Service in 1904, when it was awarded its first postal station. The government thought the name of Farewell Bend was too long, so they dropped the Farewell to make it officially Bend. The Deschutes River, however, continues its lazy wandering through the town and is still a great attraction for its citizens and visitors.

We continued through town, heading south, and about twenty miles south of Bend we turned off Highway 97 and followed the signs to East Lake and Paulina Lake in the Newberry Volcanic Monument. The Newberry National Monument was established for visitors to experience the lava, pumice, and the Big Obsidian Flow from the eruptions of ages past, but its remote location assured the minimum participation except by the most hardy, or curious. And its remoteness encouraged Sara to remind me again that we had almost one hundred fifty miles on the tank of gas we had purchased in Salem before we left the valley. But with the aplomb of a wagon master of old, I shrugged and told her not to worry, and continued up the mountain toward our destination. There was repair work being done on the roadway, and it forced us to stop once in awhile, but it did not dampen our expectation of the good time to come. The blue skies and blazing sun seemed to be much closer on the mountain than back in Portland.

By the time we arrived at the gate to the Paulina Lake camp grounds, I noticed that our gasoline gauge was showing less than a quarter of a tank. We would not have enough to drive around much, if we wanted to get back to Bend. The only solution was to hike. We needed the exercise anyway, and we loved to hike. Perhaps it was for the best. Sara almost bought that logic.

It took us about an hour to set up a camp site with our tent trailer with its side room. During times of rain, or quiet times of reading, we could sit inside the mosquito netting walls and look over the deep blue waters of Paulina Lake. We hoped we wouldn't need the protection from mosquitoes that the netting offered, but as Sara quoted to the children so many times over the years, saying, "It's better to have it and not need it, than need it and not have it!" She said this regardless of what it was she was pressing on them. In most cases she was right, and this time was no exception.

That evening, after our meal and our walk, we were sitting around our camp fire, discussing what we could do in the morning, and the mosquitoes began to take over. We moved inside the side room for protection, and to study under the lantern light the map of the surrounding area for possible hikes we could take. We could choose one of several trails that crisscrossed the region. We decided to hike to the top of Paulina Peak listed as a foot and horse trail. From up there we could get the lay of the land better. With that decision made, we were in bed before nine, tired and sleepy from the day's events, and the evening stillness.

We awoke the next morning snuggled deep in our sleeping bags, because of the cold that had swept in over the lake. We were surprised to have ice in a pan of water left out overnight. It was too cold for July, I thought, but very invigorating. The cold gave us an appetite that only the outdoors can give. The bacon and eggs Sara fixed tasted like a king's meal. The crisp bacon so sharp and salty, the fried egg so much better for you up here, even if our cholesterol was high! But it would fortify us for the hike up the mountain on Paulina Peak trail that we had agreed on the night before. We would probably wear off the effects of the breakfast before noon on the four miles up to the Peak. The trail was a two thousand foot rise, over a rock and root strewn path, and was officially a horse trail. We followed sign posts that showed the mileage, and the horseshoe insignia showed that the trail was for non-motorized traffic only.

Our nine-thirty A.M. start seemed late, but the darkness of the trail gave us the feeling that nature took her time in getting awake up here. After walking a couple of miles the sun was higher in the sky, and the rise in the trail was making us both perspire. We began searching for a log to sit on for a moment. Soon, we came upon a fork in the trail where the ground showed that horses had stood for some time. The droppings and hoof marks indicated a gathering place. One fork of the trail led toward a well-worn washboard road that no doubt gave horse trailers access for unloading. The other fork led deeper into the woods, and on up to the peak. A fallen tree provided a perfect resting place for the moment. We had to take advantage of the opportunity to sit.

After a short rest we followed the path onward and upward into the forest. About a hundred yards up the trail, there was a little worn side path to the left that led to a shelter with hitching posts and water troughs. We detoured to see what it was and came upon an overnight camp for horseback riders. It had not been used recently by the signs, probably not since late last fall. We entered into the weathered clapboard shelter by pushing against the door, constructed of rough boards nailed together, and the hinges protested loudly but allowed us to enter. The ten feet by ten feet bare planked floor, and the boarded walls that let the light through the cracks, gave us the feeling of entering a cave. There was a wood pile along one wall, a board up high for storage space on another, and a fireplace on the wall facing the door.

Sara summed up our inspection with, "Well, it is high, and it is dry! Probably a lifesaver in the winter."

With my usual banter I retorted, "Yes, but the amenities leave something to be desired, don't you think? No bunk beds, no table, nothing!"

I don't know what I expected, but the movies always made these shacks look so homey. It was a little unsettling to see that, though adequate for its purpose, it did not have the appeal that I thought it should.

As we turned to leave, Sara's eagle eye spotted something lying under a fire log that had rolled free from the pile. Going into the corner, lifting the log with my foot, we saw a brown leather billfold. We exchanged delighted glances, and I scooped it up for inspection. It was a little flattened, but no more worse for wear. I could see that it contained some bills, and the excitement of our good fortune surged through my veins. It was a brown leather ladies' billfold with a leather strap that snapped into place to hold it closed. I unsnapped it to reveal an Oregon driver's license, some credit cards, some pictures, and thirty, one hundred dollar bills. I looked at Sara, who was staring in disbelief, and I managed to mumble, "Now that's a sight for sore eyes!"

She recovered her voice to say, "I wonder how much we would get for returning it?"

But a childhood phrase was running though my mind, "Finders keepers, losers weepers!"

However, three thousand dollars was not a children's game to play! We would have to search for its owner, and return it.

2

Jimmy Perez flew from the Troutdale Airport, near Portland, to the Central Oregon Resort, which was a few miles below Bend, Oregon, on Monday, July 9th. He had scheduled a business conference with an associate who had the responsibility of distributing cocaine in the Bend area. As he flew over the Cascade Mountain Range, he marveled at how far he had advanced in his business. He had come to Los Angeles in 1972 at the age of twelve with his father, mother, and his widowed grandmother. His father had been transferred by the drug cartel from Bogota, Colombia, for the express purpose of building up a business to distribute their product in Southern California. Jose Perez, Jimmy's father, had been a very successful businessman selling farm implements in

Bogota, and had owned his own store for several years. His business had taken a severe down turn as more and more farmers turned to growing coca plants and selling their crops to the drug cartel. His alliance with the cartel, through the local "lord," gave him an opportunity to furnish the equipment used in harvesting the coca leaves for the drug. He also furnished the production equipment to extract the bitter alkaloid, cocaine.

The illegal use of cocaine for pleasure, which started in the more affluent members of the society in the United States, spread into the working class and then onto the street. The price and availability were no problems as the cartel opened up pipelines into the United States. The millions of American dollars, flowing back to them in cash, dictated the necessity for the cartel to buy businesses that could legitimize the cash, which then could be deposited into banks all over the world. The tremendous financial power of the cartel allowed them to buy the consumer outlets dealing in cash sales, as well as the banks into which the money could be deposited. The power yielded by the cartel of drug lords was even greater than the power of some of the poorer governments in South America, so it was very common that the local governments answered to the cartel.

Jose Perez purchased World Wide Sales, a company that sold and distributed heavy equipment throughout the world, with their headquarters in Los Angeles. His operation grew, aided by the cash infusion by the cartel. Jose hired and trained Jimmy in the business, and after college Jimmy went to work for him full time. Soon Jimmy was making trips to Bogota, and became familiar on how the cartel used their influence to get things done. He became part of their hierarchy by his quick wit and knowledge of the business.

Jimmy's assignment to the Great Northwest by his father to establish a sales office in the area was considered quite a feather in his cap, because of his age and the territory for which he was responsible. At the same time he was to develop drug outlets in Seattle, Portland, Boise, Helena, and in all the major resort areas throughout the four states of Washington, Oregon, Idaho, and Montana. He made his home in Portland, and since he traveled over such a wide area, he bought a company airplane. This allowed him to hop from one place to another on his time schedule, rather than the schedule of the many airlines he would have to use.

He really enjoyed flying his six passenger Cessna twin engine aircraft, and quite often mixed business and pleasure by flying into a resort area and landing on their strip for a weekend of fun and relaxation. He usually took his friend and business associate, Terry Mandano, who he had brought from Los Angeles with him. Terry was streetwise, and had been brought up to make his own way. He could handle a gun as if it were an extension of his hand, but his real expertise was with a knife. His kind of talent was necessary in Jimmy's line of business. Jimmy had a strong hold on Terry, because of the many hours invested in Terry to become a businessman, rather than the street fighter that he had been for years. Jimmy could see what a valuable asset Terry would become as a bodyguard and assistant.

Jimmy and Terry, arrived at the Central Oregon Resort's airstrip, checked out the plane, and left it for service and tie down. They were to meet with the area manager for dinner, and finish up later in the condo that Jimmy owned at the resort. Jimmy had noticed that the receipts from the Bend area had dropped off lately, and he was there to find out what the problem seemed to be.

The dinner went well. The pusher was nervous as he talked about why the business had been slower. He felt that the area, although growing from the influx of people from California, did not have the same proportion of users. Jimmy listened without too much response, except that he would check over the figures that the man had brought. If he came up with any suggestions Jimmy would get back to him.

After dinner they met again in Jimmy's office in his condo, where they made the routine exchange of merchandise for cash. Jimmy had brought the manager cocaine packets. The one hundred twenty thousand dollars exchanged was less than what Jimmy hoped, but he held his thoughts until he had a chance to check it out.

Later after their meeting, while it was still early, Jimmy announced that he and Terry were going bike riding early the next morning, and excused himself to get to bed early. Jimmy had established long ago that his body would always be in the utmost physical condition. This dictated the correct amount of sleep, the maximum amount of exercise, and only the best and the most nutritious food to eat.

Jimmy and Terry rode their well-equipped mountain bikes out of the Central Oregon Resort area before the sun had topped the trees. They headed south on Highway 97 for about ten miles to the turn-off to Paulina Lake and East Lake. A recently installed sign at the turn-off heralded the establishment of the Newberry National Volcanic Monument and depicted the fifty-eight thousand acres of lava and obsidian flows that were enveloped in its boundaries. The road wound its way for fourteen miles up the mountain to the two lakes situated near the base of the 7,985 feet high Paulina Peak, which was the highest of the Paulina Mountains that ringed the lakes. The lakes sit in the caldera of what once was Mount Newberry, which blew its top thousands of years ago, spewing the lava and obsidian flows for man to ponder in awe at their wonders.

On this day the two bikers, who were outfitted and equipped for the long ride, needed all the strength and endurance they could muster to make the twenty-five hundred feet rise in the road over the fourteen miles to the lakes. There were places where the pavement was broken up from the winter freezing, and there were other places where it had washed out entirely and was under repair. The frequent detours and constant awareness to the road condition caused frequent rest stops, and drinks from water bottles strapped to the frames of their bikes.

By nine-thirty A.M. they reached the Paulina Lake campgrounds. Terry had not discussed with Jimmy where they were going to ride for the day. He had decided that he would go wherever Jimmy led him, and today's ride was a combination of a test of endurance and a challenge to his senses. He could not believe the vastness of the forest, and its stillness and solitude. It compared, somewhat, to flying with Jimmy in his airplane. The panorama from the plane, the aloneness one felt, the detached feeling he had at ten thousand feet were very similar feelings he had as he rode through forested canyons, and by the loud rushing waters of the cascading waterfalls. He liked the feeling of exerting his muscles until they ached for relief, and to ride to the top of a hill and around a bend to witness another vista of beauty or another challenge of strength. The sense of accomplishment he received from a long ride was like nothing else. It was almost as good as winning a street fight with a worthy foe. Jimmy probably would never understand that feeling. He and Jimmy could share the other feelings, though, and often did.

Jimmy Perez had his own personal thoughts as he rode and pushed himself to the limit of endurance. He enjoyed the exertion, also, but on this day he was on a reconnoitering trip through an area where he had only been once before. He wanted to make sure that what he remembered of the area was how it actually was. The vast forests, the beautiful lakes, the wild animals, the high flying hawks, and the gurgle of the streams cascading down the mountain were in themselves worth the trip. His purpose, today, was to set his mind at rest concerning the area around the obsidian flow. His fascination with the flow, and the area around it, was like a magnet for his thoughts. He believed his fascination was because of the absolute isolation, and the desolation in black and gray that was situated in the middle of a forest of green and blue.

It was similar to parts of his body. He thought of how perfectly shaped his shoulders, upper arms, and thighs were. They should be, he thought, because he spent so much time keeping them that way. However, there were parts of his body that he just could not make to look perfect. His lower arms to him looked to be all knots and lumps. It may have come from too many arm lifts, too many strains, or too much weight lifting. Whatever the cause for this imperfection, in his mind it was a blight on the otherwise perfect body makeup. This is how he viewed the Obsidian Flow below Paulina Peak, which was a blotch in an otherwise perfect setting.

The two men rested at the Paulina campground for only fifteen minutes until they continued up the road toward East Lake, four miles away. About halfway to the lake there was an entry to a parking lot for the Obsidian Flow Observatory. By following the trail signs one could follow the path onto the flow, and continue to follow the path as it wound around and through the flow. The path circled through a portion of the flow, and then back to the starting point near the parking lot. This path had been laid out by the Forest Service so the wonders of the flow could be seen and appreciated up close. Thousands of visitors had visited this portion of the flow each year since it was established in 1990.

The two bikers, however, detoured around the flow, and followed a trail upward toward the top of Paulina Peak. The mountain of black shiny glassy rock and the gray boulders were over fifty feet high and impregnable. Keeping the flow on their left, they finally came to a spot where they thought they could climb up to the top of the flow. The shale-like obsidian cascaded down the side of the flow as they tried to scramble upward. They risked slicing their legs and ankles, but finally scrambled over the top, and stood looking over the flow.

The view that they scanned was not unlike the surface of a giant table with every inch covered with broken and jagged glass. No human had ever walked across it at that spot, and probably never would. Deep fissures that looked like dark caves challenged the imagination to determine their depth. This inhospitable terrain stretched out for several hundred yards, and was said to be very unstable. Beautiful to look at, but not recommended for travelers.

After a few minutes, the two bikers descended the flow, following the zig-zag route that they had used climbing up the side, and continued on up the trail. The trail followed the flow until the sides of the flow blended into the mountain side where it all had started. They could easily climb onto the flow from this spot and look back down as it progressed toward the lakes. The sun glistened off the black rocks, like shimmering diamonds across the ground, but the bikers paused for just a moment before continuing.

The trail continued up the mountain to the top. It was a very difficult trip for the bikers. The trail was rock strewn, and the exposed roots of the trees growing along the side of the trail made it almost impossible to ride. The bikers pushed the bikes for long stretches, and as they gained altitude would stop at a clearing to rest. The obsidian dominated the landscape below, as it stretched out down toward the lakes. Jimmy's interest in the landscape was very clinical in its approach. He viewed the terrain as if it was under a microscope. He searched each crevice and void, and moved his examination to a new sector on his mind's grid only after cataloging the location of each foot of the old sector. Terry watched him with great interest as he peered intently at the black expanse. Terry often wondered what Jimmy was thinking when his friend studied an object with such intense curiosity. He probably would never know, however, since Jimmy kept most thoughts to himself.

They reached the top of the peak by eleven thirty, had a sandwich and a drink from their bottles, rested for a few minutes, then pushed off down the trail that led to Paulina Lake campgrounds, four miles away by the trail.

3

Sara and I looked at each other with raised eyebrows. There were a lot of questions concerning the billfold in my hands. We had some digging to do if we were to find the answers to our questions. We both had an overwhelming desire to get out of the shelter and tear into the information the wallet held. We went outside and sat on a log, feeling that we were being watched even though there was no one around. The sounds of the forest became a little louder. A tree rubbing against another suddenly took on an ominous sound. The breeze that was stirring in the trees seemed to be covering the sounds that I was straining to hear. It was as if we had stolen something from a church! We felt like intruders in this time and space. Guilty conscience? Maybe. More likely a premonition of what was to come from that wallet.

Sara took out the drivers license and looked at the face of a woman whose beauty came through, even in that picture. She was born May 10th, 1961, blond hair, 5'4," 120 lbs., with green eyes, according to the statistics shown. Her name was Cindy M. Johnson. Address was 7420 Ridge Rim Drive, Portland, Oregon. We looked at each other. That address was close to where we lived in Portland! She probably had gone to the same high school as our youngest child, Shelly, who was born in 1961 also. Wouldn't it be a coincidence if they knew each other?

The Visa credit card and the library card were in the same name. A picture of Cindy and a young man depicted the pair standing on the bridge of a sailboat. Cindy was posed as the captain and he a crew member. I took it from Sara and turned the picture over. On the back there was a notation, "Ron, July 1990." The only other item of interest was a business card from "Across the Seas Travel Agency" with the name "Sue Rominger" blazoned in golden script-type printing. On each corner there were swaying palm trees with the sun peeking through their branches.

"A very nice business card," Sara mused. "Three colors, two types of script, and special printing. Based on the cards you had in your previous position, this looks expensive!"

"Like I always said, if you have it, flaunt it!" I said, laughingly. "But we never had it to flaunt!"

Sara just smiled and placed all the pieces back into the wallet.

"Let's try returning it when we get back to Portland," she said.

"Should be fairly easy to do," I returned, "since we have all her ID. Besides, what could we do with three thousand dollars? Too much to spend foolishly, and too little to save."

"Well, I wouldn't say that!" Sara said. "Let's just return it when we get back. I would like to meet a person who carries that kind of money while hiking in the wilds."

"Me too," I said, as I shoved myself off the log. "Let's

continue our hike. We'll talk about it on the way up to the top. It's going to be lunchtime when we get there."

Sara agreed and stuffed the wallet deep in a zippered pocket on the backpack I was carrying. We had about two miles to go to the top, four miles to come down on our hike today, and we had all the rest of the week for hiking, swimming, and camping before we could do anymore about our little find.

Looking around the trail camp as we started to leave, it was interesting to see how preserved the feed trough and corral were. The trough was about twenty feet long and three feet high. It was a foot wide at the bottom, and with a two feet opening at the top, somewhat like a *V*. There were six stalls for horses attached to the trough. The stalls were little more than a pair of rails spaced two feet high, an opening approximately three and one-half feet wide, and ten feet long. Horses could stand and feed from the trough, while separated from each other. Although there were a couple of rails that had become unattached, the wood was in fairly good condition. The feeding arrangement, and the overall condition of the corral, looked well maintained in spite of their age.

From the riders' camp upward, the trail was starting to get interesting, and it began to get steeper as it ascended to the seventy-nine foot level. The scenery was changing faster, also. It was getting even more spectacular. Our hike was much harder with more frequent stops to rest and catch our breath. As the trail became more narrow and more steep, the frequent stops gave us a chance to take in the view.

It was a panoramic collage of snow-capped mountains, deep blue lakes, and tall firs. The firs stood like sentinels guarding the access to all the mountains possessed. Below and off to the right to the northeast the obsidian flow stretched out two miles long and a mile wide. The shining black boulders and gray cinders formed an almost impassable barrier. From this distance the flow looked like a raised growth on the flesh of Paulina Peak.

Onward and upward at a slower pace we trudged through

thinning pine. At the seven thousand foot level we began to see snow drifts that existed even on an eighty-five degree day. They were protected from the direct sunlight and melted very slowly. The small tricklets that flowed from the melting snow down the trail caused soft muddy spots that we had to detour. There didn't seem to have been any other hikers up the trail this morning, and our tracks on the snowdrifts that we had to cross gave us a feeling of isolation. We knew that there was an unpaved gravel road only about a mile away that ascended to the observatory at the top, but the feeling of isolation came from the stillness and the vastness of the scenery.

The trail was maintained by the U.S. Forest Service personnel of the Deschutes National Forest. The Forest Service oversees all the national forests in Oregon to assure the multiple use of the natural resources within their boundaries. Including the Deschutes National Forest, nearly fifty percent of Oregon's land mass was covered by national forests. In the Cascade Mountain Range there were the Deschutes, Mount Hood, the Willamette, the Rogue, the Winema, and the Fremont National Forests. Within their borders were the scenic wonders such as Crater Lake National Park, several wildlife refuges, wilderness areas, and lakes of different sizes and depths. To stand and look as far as one could see, and try to take in the vastness of the landscape was a thrilling and inspiring adventure that anyone could participate in. The federal government has the charge to maintain it from abuses from all users, whether they be recreational, industrial, or political. It was a most difficult job, requiring the wisdom of Solomon.

As we came nearer to the top we met our first fellow travelers on the trail. We had to move quickly off to the side of the trail to allow two bicyclers right of way as they came hurtling down the trail on their mountain bikes. They came to a not very controlled stop, sliding on the loose rocks on the trail, and raising a cloud of dust.

"Hello!" the first man exclaimed. His smile revealed the most even white teeth that I had ever seen. He was a muscular fellow and his black net T-shirt did nothing but emphasize that fact. His traveling companion was smaller, but looked in excellent shape.

"Hi!" we both chimed. "You have a long rough trail ahead downward on those bikes. How did you come up?" I asked.

"We came up and around the Obsidian Flow. We had to walk our bikes in some places, but it was worth it when we got to the top. Is there anything interesting to see along the trail on the way up?" the smaller man asked in a quiet voice.

"There is a horse camp at the six thousand foot level, but that's about it," I said. I did not want them to know about our "find."

"Did you camp at one of the lakes last night?" I wondered.

"No, we came over from the Central Oregon Resort," said "Smiley," underplaying the fact that it was at least twenty miles away.

"You are having quite a ride this morning!" Sara stated, duly impressed. "You better watch it going down on this trail. There is a log placed across the trail at various spots to channel the water from melting snow away from the trail. If you hit one it would be disastrous!"

"We'll keep it in mind," said the second biker as they pushed off down the trail with a wave. "Have a good hike!"

We watched as they went cascading down the trail, rocks careening away as they loosened beneath the wheels of their bikes. At that rate they would cover the distance we had walked in a fraction of the time. If they lived through it, that is. I was still marveling at the route they had covered this morning, and at the same time resentful that they made it look so easy. The trails around the obsidian flow and up the other side of the mountain looked liked a very strenuous ride. They had to get up very early to ride twenty miles, then ride across the bottom of the flow and then up the other side. They must have really enjoyed mountain biking!

When we got to the top, we were surprised to see several cars that were parked in the parking lot. The drivers had endured the unpaved and rutted gravel road that leads up from the campgrounds. Their presence, however, did not take away the fabulous view from the perch we had chosen to sit and eat our lunches. We sat on an outcropping of rock as close to the top of the seventy-nine hundred foot high mountain as we could get. As we scanned the horizon, we could see eight snow-capped mountains. We could see the Three Sisters Mountains to the northwest; namely, the North Sister, the Middle Sister, and the South Sister. They all stood stately, proud, and over ten thousand feet high. From this distance their peaks almost blended together with Mt. Bachelor, Broken Top, and Mt. Washington which rose up to nearly eight thousand feet, but twenty-five miles farther to the northwest. Mt. Jefferson and Three Finger Jack showed their mantles of white seventy-five miles more to the north, and still farther north Mt. Hood at over eleven thousand feet, regally ruling over them all.

To make the panorama of nature still more breathtaking were the green forests carpeting the foothills, the blue lakes nestled in the valleys, and to the south more of the same that stretched out as far as you could see. There were areas without roads that were only accessible by foot or horseback. As we gazed below us we could follow the road from Paulina Lake around the lake and the end of the lava flow and on to East Lake. My eye automatically tried to follow the biker's route around the flow and up the trail, but gave it up when I heard Sara speak. She was peering down toward the Paulina Lake campgrounds where we had started.

"That horse camp and shelter was about there," she said as she pointed where the mountain increased its pitch, and near a cut in the trees where the unpaved road came close to the trail.

"I can't understand why she would have lost her billfold in that place, can you?" she asked.

"No, I can't," I murmured. I'd almost forgotten about the "find."

"I suppose she just dropped it getting some firewood from the pile," I mumbled, having no way of knowing.

We sat on our perch for maybe half an hour, looking at the view. We could see other lava flows just a few miles to the north. When we looked at our maps, it showed in that area the Lava Cast Forest, Lava River Caves State Park, Arnold Ice Caves, and Lava Butte. This area was certainly picturesque, and it was hard to leave a place where we could take it in with a sweep of our eyes.

After we had eaten our lunch and stuffed our debris into our pack, we pointed out some sights to some people sitting in a car with New York license plates. We talked for a while, and headed back down the same trail we had ascended. Our trip down, although harder on our knees and thighs from bracing ourselves against sliding on loose rocks, was much faster. We arrived back at the guard shack at the entrance to the campgrounds in about an hour and a half.

As we approached the campground we saw the two bikers we had met on the trail. They were lounging on a picnic table where they could see everyone coming into the camp from the road, or from the trail. I had a feeling they were waiting for us. As we approached, they waved and strolled over to meet us. The one with the broad shoulders and beautiful white teeth that gleamed against his tanned face spoke first.

"Well, how was the view up there? Did you enjoy the hike?" he asked.

"Eight miles is a long hike for a guy like me who is not in the shape he should be. I wouldn't even try the trip you guys took," I answered, trying to show my admiration for what they had done. If I was hoping for an a compliment back for our accomplishment, which I felt was just a little more than a Sunday stroll through the park, I was disappointed.

The larger one of the two asked, "Did you see anything, uh…special from up there?"

"Yeah, isn't it great? It was so clear we could see several mountains, including Mt. Hood," I said. "We took a series of pictures in a three-hundred-and-sixty-degree-panoramic sweep. I hope it comes out. The Obsidian Flow and East Lake shot was the best one, I think."

"Are you staying at Paulina or East Lake campground?" asked the larger man.

"Here at Paulina Lake. The camp ground is a little more shielded from the wind off the lake here," Sara answered.

"Where are you from?" he asked, continuing his questioning in a friendly manner.

"Portland," I said. "And you?"

"Portland, also," he answered.

"Where are you staying?" I asked.

"Central Oregon Resort," he answered with a big smile. "We rented these bikes there. How long are you staying?"

"Probably until Saturday," Sara chimed in.

We talked a couple of minutes, and Sara suggested we go on into our camp. We said goodbye, and they mounted their bikes as we headed back to our campsite. I had the feeling of being questioned about something I had no knowledge of, or at least I hoped not. I also hoped I didn't cross their paths again. They gave me an uncomfortable feeling which I could not explain.

4

Jimmy and Terry mounted their bikes, after the old couple they had spoken to walked into the campgrounds, and pushed off to return to the Central Oregon Resort. They would probably make the return trip in a couple of hours, being at the condo by three thirty or four o'clock. Jimmy lapsed into concentrating on his trip to Boise the next day. He was to meet one of his associates for lunch at the airport Holiday Inn, so he would have to fly out early. It was very difficult for him to spend time riding bicycles in the Cascades, but he had to get away from business now and then. Besides, this ride to the flow had to be made. He had to refresh his memory on the lay of the land around the lakes. It was pretty much as he had remembered it. There seemed to be several visitors this year to the mountain. They could mess up the whole area, he grumbled to himself. Just think, that old couple hiked up the trail that Terry and he had just come down. If they could hike that far, younger people could go farther, and stay longer without horses even. His secrets in the area would someday be revealed, but the longer the better.

The bikers made good time riding back to their condo. It was downhill almost all the way, but it had been a full day and both men were ready for a shower and a rest before dinner. Jimmy immediately took a long shower, and then lay down on the bed in his room, thinking of what he was going to do tomorrow. He thought that it would be a good idea to leave Terry here at the condo while he made the trip to Boise. He could fly on to a couple of other places to deliver some merchandise to his associates, and be back in a couple of days.

In the meantime, Terry could pick up a rental car and drive over to the Mountain View Resort, and then up to the Cascade Ski Resort and make deliveries. He could meet with their associate in Bend again and discuss the possibility of higher sales there. Jimmy felt that his man in Bend was too nervous when they met the night before. He also felt that sales should be at least twenty-five percent higher. Terry could "encourage" him to crank up sales a little, by putting a little "pressure" on the pusher. Then Jimmy and Terry could meet back here on Friday, go over what they had accomplished, and tally the cash brought back.

At dinner that night Jimmy went over the plans he had made with Terry. They felt it was a good sales trip for both of them, and should bring in over five hundred thousand dollars for the four-day trip. Terry asked only one question during the evening. He wanted a feel for how much "pressure" should be applied to their pusher in Bend. Jimmy left no doubt of what he had in mind. His instructions were to use whatever force was necessary to get the job done. If the man was laid up from the injuries that he might sustain in their discussions, however, sales may fall until a replacement can be found. Terry smiled his approval of his instructions, and looked forward to his meeting with the pusher later in the week.

Terry always felt much better when he was allowed to use his talents of persuasion. Jimmy used words to persuade others to do his will, but Terry believed his methods were easier to understand. And if things got out of hand, the situation could always be rectified by installing another associate in the unpersuaded's place. The reluctant pusher's body would turn up someday as another statistic in the drug war. Business would go on as before, through a more willing and more pliable peddler.

Jimmy's Cessna lifted off the ground from the Central Oregon Resort's airstrip at ten A.M., flew due east to Boise, and he walked into Boise's Airport Holiday Inn's dining room at noon to meet with his local area manager. He was greeted by a well-dressed man of fifty with silver white hair, jovial smile, and jowls and double chin that met somewhere under the rolls of fat that made up his neck. He wore a suit that spoke of money, and it aided in the illusion that he was thinner than he actually was. The friendly aura that he cast reminded Jimmy of a used car dealer he once knew. In fact, that was Sam Stuckard's former profession. He owned Friendly Sam's Auto Sales and Repair in Boise, before Jimmy made him a deal he could not refuse. Now, he distributed cocaine to the pushers in town, and across Idaho into Utah as far as Salt Lake City. He received a cut of every sale, and Sam knew how to sell a product.

Jimmy waved him to remain seated, shook his hand and took a seat across the table facing Sam. By shifting his eyes only slightly he could watch nearly everyone entering and leaving the restaurant. It was something Jimmy always did, because he did not like surprise happenings behind him.

They talked as they ate, Jimmy eating a very light fare, but Sam ate as he usually did, enough for two people. Between bites Sam filled Jimmy in on how well his area was doing in sales. The briefcase at his feet contained reports, statistics on each of his pushers, and money for the merchandise Jimmy had brought. Both carried identical briefcases.

The luncheon and the business were completed when Jimmy finished his tea, and Sam had finished his coffee and pie. They shook hands again, Sam placed a twenty in the tray with the check for lunch, and handed it to the waitress. Jimmy picked up Sam's briefcase in exchange for the one he brought, and both men left the restaurant each carrying over one hundred and fifty thousand dollars. Jimmy had cash, Sam had merchandise. Both headed in different directions. Jimmy took a taxi back to the airstrip. He did not want to linger longer than necessary after the switch had been made.

Meanwhile, the morning's work had gone well for Terry Mandano. He had driven the forty-five miles to the Mountain View Resort. His meeting was to take place at lunch also at the dining room at the lodge. His luncheon date was Sandy Simpson, a very attractive brunette, well dressed in a business suit that emphasized all the right places, and hid those that she did not want shown. She was strictly business in her approach, but had a face that got her noticed. She met Terry as he entered the lodge, and they both walked up the steps to the dining room. They were seated in a booth that took in the view of the meadow and the lake. Terry was rather ill at ease, but soon warmed to Sandy as she talked about how much she liked living and working here at the lodge. Her relationship with Jimmy had only recently been established, but it had been a lucrative association to date. Her position as assistant to the business manager in charge of corporate bookings had given her access to buyers of cocaine that they used for pleasure. She had been approached by businessmen to find out where they could buy, long before she was in position to sell. She could supply other entertainment that they were willing to pay for, because there was a ready supply of young women she knew. But for herself, she did not participate. The money she made from selling the merchandise was sufficient to keep her in the manner she had always wanted.

They had lunch and the small talk was pleasant and

relaxing. Terry really enjoyed himself, and vowed to come back sometime when he could spend more time to get to know this self-assured woman. She made him feel like she was interested in what he was saying, although most of his conversation was about what he and Jimmy did together.

After lunch he made the exchange of briefcases, which was the method that Jimmy had set up. She had informed him of the amount she had placed in her briefcase, and knew that the packets of white powder in his briefcase was the amount she had ordered. The fifty thousand dollars in his case would be tallied with the other when he and Jimmy met on Friday.

He drove back to Bend and stopped in at the Cascade Dining Room that was situated on the east bank of the Deschutes River near Drake Park, and according to the advertisements, catered to only the most discerning clientele. He asked for John Hickman, the manager, the man he and Jimmy had met with only two nights before at the Central Oregon Resort. John came out of his office and greeted Terry, and the puzzled look on his face asked the question even before he asked it. Terry asked him what time he could meet for a talk concerning some things that Jimmy had questioned, upon reflection, after their meeting the other night. Hickman agreed to meet around four at his place east of town. Hickman drew a map on the back of his card, wrote his address, and handed it to Terry. Terry accepted it with thanks and said he would meet with him at four o'clock, which was in about two hours.

After a couple more stops, Terry drove out to the address he had been given. It was a small ranch, with a house that had been built recently with all the modern amenities found in the better neighborhoods. He drove past the driveway entrance to the ranch house, and did not stop. He wanted to see the route in and out of the area, before he parked his car. He drove along the painted white fences of the ranches along the road, turned at the first crossroad, and followed the pavement to the intersection with the highway into Bend. He turned around and went back to the intersection not far from John Hickman's ranch, turned on the road that bordered it, and parked in a wayside park that consisted of a tree for shade, and a picnic table. He remained in his car, but kept the house under surveillance from about three hundred yards away.

When Hickman drove into the long driveway up to the house, Terry could see that he was alone. Terry hesitated until he saw Hickman walk to the door with his key out to unlock it. Terry surmised that there was no one to greet him, neither a wife nor a dog. He started his engine and drove into the driveway and up to the house. His ring of the door chime brought Hickman immediately, who invited him in and led him to an office in the rear of the house.

After entering the office ahead of Terry, Hickman turned to offer him a seat on a leather sofa along one wall facing the desk. Terry's chopping blow with the edge of his hand was to Hickman's neck, and the man crumbled like a rag doll onto the sofa, with his face down and half his body on the floor. Terry leaned over, lifted Hickman's legs like the handles of a wheelbarrow, and tossed him into a lying position onto the sofa. He bent down, felt for a pulse at Hickman's outstretched wrist, and left the man to sleep while Terry checked out his office.

Hickman kept good records. They were too good. In the lap drawer of his solid oak desk, which had been locked until Terry forced it open, was a ledger showing the transactions and sales dollars he had reported to Jimmy and him at the meeting. Terry scanned the entries and laid the ledger open on the desk. He reached over and flipped the switch on the computer on the desk. When the menu came up, he selected the Lotus 1-2-3 program and searched the directory until he found the file he wanted. The income for the past six months was about twenty-five percent higher than the entries for the same periods on the ledger. The expenses listed in the file revealed that most of the excess income was being spent on his ranch, with considerable amounts into stock equities that were listed in a separate file.

Terry turned the printer on and made hard copies of the

three files that condemned Hickman to show Jimmy. Just as the last document was printed, he heard a groan and a stirring from the sofa. He placed the printouts in his jacket inside pocket, shut down the computer and printer, and walked around the desk to sit on a guest chair facing the sofa. When Hickman's eyes flickered open to see Terry sitting casually in the chair, fear leaped into his eyes, and he came to a sitting position slowly. Terry took the printouts from his jacket pocket, and without a word moved closer so that Hickman could see the printing. Sheer panic crossed Hickman's face as he realized what secrets Terry had uncovered. He pushed himself away from the sofa, lunged with outstretched hands for Terry's neck, but was hammered back with a chop to his throat with Terry's bent fingers. Terry forced Hickman's face into a pillow, and held it until Hickman went limp. Terry grinned at the knowledge that the man would never enjoy his stolen wealth again.

Terry cleaned up any evidence of his presence there and slipped out the front door. He got into his rented car, drove out of the circular driveway, and headed on to the Cascade Ski Resort for his last delivery.

5

After our hike and a rest, Sara and I walked around the edge of Lake Paulina from our campsite to a boat landing and a pier nearby. There were several boats brought in for the evening and tied up to the walkway perpendicular to the pier. Sitting back further away from the lake was a small building that doubled as a boat rental and grocery store. Across the road and up the lake about two hundred yards was a lodge with a restaurant. It was a two-story building made from logs, and the word that best described it politely was quaint. Behind the lodge was a horse corral with four horses and a stable. We saw a man attending the horses, so we walked over to speak to him. As we got closer we recognized him as the cowboy we had seen in the restaurant in Sisters on the way from Portland.

"Hi! What beautiful horses. Do you rent them for trail riding?" I asked, stating the obvious, and feeling a little foolish for asking since I had no intention of renting one.

"Yep," he drawled without missing a stroke at brushing down a beautiful brown and white Appaloosa stallion. "The day rate is twenty dollars an hour without guide, one hundred dollar minimum. Three day outings are four hundred fifty dollars with guide and everything included. Weekly rates with pack horses are available for two or more people. Interested?" He looked at us doubtfully, figuring us for the city folks out for an evening stroll that we were.

"No, thank you," I said, leaning on the fence railing. "We are better suited for walking at our age, I think."

"Oh, I don't know," said the weathered face handler. "We get them all ages and sizes. Lot of first timers on day rates. Makes them feel the Old West clear down in their bones, where it counts." He smiled and his teeth were stained from either chewing tobacco, or too much black coffee on the trail. Probably it was a little of both! His hat looked as old as he was, and stained around the hat band. The Old West would never be dead while he was still kicking!

He pulled out a business card from a wallet, and handed it to me. It read "Shorty Hobson," and underneath "Trail Horse Rentals." I took it, more from courtesy than anything, and said that I would pass it around to interested parties back in Portland. I put it in my wallet to save as a discussion starter sometime.

We walked on over to the lodge and entered the front door. We stepped directly into the dining room. Six tables were made up with service for four. The blue checkered table cloths were clean and neatly ironed with matching napkins neatly folded. The curtains were also freshly done, and it made the atmosphere as warm and inviting as any restaurant you could find.

The woman who came through a doorway from the back rooms was heavyset with a smile as big as she was. Her friendly, "Hello!" greeting gave us a feeling of being truly welcome.

"Hi!" Sara responded. "We don't want to eat with you tonight, but we may later in the week. Do you have a menu we could look at? We are camped over in the campgrounds, and before the week is out John may get tired of campfire food."

"Lots of people do that. Here is one you can have to take with you. Our daily specials are listed for the whole week."

We made small talk by asking how long she had been running this place. She told us about her and Shorty owning their own ranch up until three years ago. They sold it and came up here to retire, doing what they enjoyed. Her restaurant looked like a farmhouse dining room, and one could tell she enjoyed what she was doing.

We talked for a while, thanked her, and left to continue our walk. The sun was setting and the shimmering gleam off the lake was beautiful. We walked down to the pier where a few boats were tied up on each side. There were canoes for rent that were pulled up on the beach. Their aluminum hulls gleamed in the setting sun. It all looked too commercial for that area, but with the number of fishermen that fished the lake, I could see why it was all necessary, and could be a lot of fun.

Paulina Lake, pronounced by the locals as Paul-i-na, was fairly large by anyone's standard. It was almost seven and a half miles around, and was alive with fish. The water was a deep blue. The trees came almost to the water's edge, leaving very little sandy beach. There were outcropping of large rocks that allowed fishermen to stand and cast. Even at dusk there were several boats with fishermen still trying to catch their supper. We were enchanted by the beauty of the scene as the setting sun began to disappear behind the tree covered mountain ridge across the lake. The beauty of Paulina Lake, Paulina Peak, the surrounding Paulina Mountains, and Paulina Creek certainly belied their namesake. Chief Paulina, a marauding Snake Indian of the Cascades during the 1850's, nearly drove the early settlers crazy by stealing their cattle and horses. He was quite a tactician, however, and outmaneuvered his pursuers for several years. His name left on the area's land mark was a tribute to his skills in outwitting the white men of his time.

During the next couple of days we spent hiking to the Obsidian Flow Observatory, and on trails in the surrounding area. The Forest Service had carved out a trail through a portion of the flow, furnishing access to points of interest within the flow. Along the path they had placed signs noting the more unique exhibits of strange and wonderful aspects of the flow. I remember seeing one of the many holes that had been created by lava flowing in a wave, so that the top of the wave had rolled over and touched the flow leaving a void. How deep, or how long the caves actually measured, was sometimes impossible to tell. We could see nothing past the first ten or so feet into them. The signs continued to remind hikers to stay on the trail. They really didn't have to remind us, it was hard enough just climbing up the trail. To climb over the broken obsidian boulders would be too much like climbing on glass. One slip and it could mean a very serious cut or scrape.

It all seemed so stark and barren without any green growth throughout the flow. With so much greenery in the background it emphasized the absence of life. It was a rare plant that could survive in that barren landscape. It would be a rare animal that would stay on top and survive for long, but there were innumerable places for them to hide.

We spent one day hiking to Paulina Falls, which were formed by Paulina Creek. The creek flows out of the lake and cascades down the mountain, cutting a deep gorge with one hundred feet high vertical cliffs in some places. Paulina Falls were actually two falls side by side, falling one hundred feet over a sheer cliff, causing a shimmering spray in the sunlight. The Forest Service had built a platform below the falls to view the spectacle, placing camera buffs in position to record the splendor.

We stood there soaking up the scene and the spray for some time, before hiking back to camp. The trail was high up on the bank overlooking the creek. The deer and other wildlife had to come down that same trail to get to the water in certain places. So our hike that day was slower than usual, because we would stop to see the deer before they would bound down the almost vertical hillside to the stream below. It occurred to me that as beautiful as this country was, it could be just as dangerous as it was pretty. The difference between life and death was a narrow trail, and one must walk it to stay alive.

The final day was a hike around the lake. We barely made it all the way, because my feet were just too sore to hike much more. We had covered over twenty-eight miles in four days over some pretty harsh terrain. Sara did not complain about her feet, so I figured she did not suffer any problems. I would probably hear about my malingering for a few days from Sara, but the day was so beautiful, I only wanted to lounge around camp reading and relaxing. And so did she.

We had really enjoyed ourselves, taking pictures of the fantastic scenery, enjoying the peaceful evenings, hiking the trails, and climbing to the top to survey the world around. We both would enjoy getting back to Portland and the routine by tomorrow night. We were also looking forward to returning the wallet we had found. It could be quite rewarding.

We broke camp the next morning, Saturday morning, and were out of the park by ten fifteen. I had not been able to buy any gas from the boat rental office at Paulina or East Lake, so we would have to coast downhill and conserve our fuel as much as possible. We came into Bend on fumes, feeling very fortunate to have made it. The two hundred thirty miles was more than I could believe possible for that old gas guzzler, while pulling a trailer.

We stopped in Sisters for lunch at the Crossing, which was packed with summer tourists. The streets of Sisters were crawling with people participating in Quilt Day. There were hand sewn quilts on display in almost every place of business along the main street. It made the town seem like the midway of a carnival, where there was something for everyone to see.

We had to wait a few minutes for a table at the Crossing, and as we stood taking in the decor, Sara nudged me and whispered, "Look who just came in," gazing to her right toward the door.

"Well, look who's here," I mumbled. I had recognized the bicycler with the broad shoulders and toothy smile immediately. I turned and nodded just as we were greeted by the waitress, asking if we would like the booth in the corner. We agreed, and were seated.

"Isn't that a coincidence, meeting those two guys here?" Sara pondered.

"Quite a coincidence," I stated. "Especially when you consider Paulina Peak is at least sixty miles from here. This is not the only restaurant in town, and we haven't seen them for three days."

As we left the restaurant I ambled over to their table and said chidingly, "Hey! You guys following us?" I offered my hand with a smile to Mr. Broad Shoulders, and nodded to his partner.

"Sure," he said, and took my hand. "How was your vacation?"

"Really great," Sara said. "We covered a lot of ground during the week. We hiked up Paulina, to the flow, to the falls, around the lake, and took some great pictures."

"How was your vacation?" she asked.

"We covered a lot of territory, also. Great fun," he said looking at his friend, who nodded in agreement. They seemed a little uncomfortable talking to us, so we exchanged a few more pleasantries about our time in the Cascades, then said goodbye and left. We headed for home, leaving an area that we had enjoyed, and looked forward to when we could return.

Saturday evening after we had rested from bringing the luggage in, cleaning out the trailer, and cleaning up, Sara said it would be a good time to call Cindy Johnson. We could set up a time for us to meet with her, and return her wallet. I looked in the phone book, and sure enough, there was her name at the address on her license. I dialed her number, and a young women's voice answered.

"Hello," I stammered out, "my name is John. I would like to speak with Cindy Johnson, if she is there, please." I heard a sharp intake of breath from the receiver.

"She isn't here. What is this all about?" the voice quivered as she spoke. Her doubt of my sincerity came through her voice, and flags shot up in my mind to go slower.

"Well," I said hesitantly, "we have found a billfold with her I.D. in it, and I would like to return it to her."

A long pause, then the voice stammered out, "She has been missing since last fall. The police would be quite interested in when and where you found it."

"Oh! That's terrible! I'm sorry to hear that! Has there been a police investigation?" I asked quietly.

"Yes," she said, with a full quiver in her voice now. "Ask for a Sergeant Phil Hansen. He has been out asking questions, and following up on things."

"Thank you," I stammered. "Are you a relative?"

"No," she said. Her voice was so low I could hardly hear. "I am her roommate. We were—are best friends." Her voice broke again, so I thanked her and told her that I hoped the police would soon find where her roommate had gone.

I put the phone down with an unsteady hand, shaken by the turn of the events. Our little holiday had opened up a can of worms. An unsolved missing person case. And to think that we might be able to shed some light on it!

I thought to myself, "Missing persons." That is an odd phrase. People who are not where they are supposed to be. A child who has gone astray, or a father who has taken off, or a mother who leaves without a trace. These may be missing persons, but when there is a connotation of possible foul play, they become more than just "missing."

It would be interesting to follow this situation to its conclusion.

6

After leaving Boise, Idaho, Jimmy flew to Walla Walla, Washington and spent the night in a motel near the airport. He had a nine A.M. appointment with his area manager, Hank Timmons. Hank had lived in the area all of his forty-two years. He had been wounded in Vietnam, which resulted in the amputation of his right leg. It had been fitted with a prosthesis, and as he walked there was only a faint limp. His walk had not been affected by the wound as much as his attitude on life. His face did not show the burning hatred inside, down low in his stomach. His face did not show much of anything. The emotionless expression and his dull gray eyes, that looked at the world as if it was something that had to be tolerated, gave him an aura of superiority. A hard man to like, and someone you would not want to cross. At six feet three inches tall, two hundred ten pounds, and firm around the belt, he was an imposing figure with whom to contend.

Jimmy sat in a booth overlooking the parking lot, and saw Timmons drive up in his 4x4 long cab Dodge. He parked away from other cars straddling the line to take up two parking places, and as he got out Jimmy saw him reach back for his Stetson. He jammed it on his head pulling the brim down low over his eyes. He was dressed in a light gray western-cut suit, and cowboy boots that glistened in the morning sun. He lifted out of the back of the extended cab a briefcase that matched Jimmy's, and strode into the restaurant. Ignoring the receptionist, he looked toward Jimmy, took off his Stetson, and strode to the booth with an outstretched hand. Jimmy took his hand and waved him into the seat across the table. A touch of a smile came over Hank's face, and Jimmy realized that he had been honored with one of Hank's few smiles of the day.

They talked about how business in the area had been steady with very little increase in the past six months. Hank surmised that it was probably due to the layoffs that had hit the area in the timber industry, construction, and cattle. It seemed that nearly all the industries that brought in the high paying jobs were slow, and might be that way for a long time. He had expanded his sales area to pick up some of the cities in the surrounding territory. He was covering as far down as La Grande, Oregon, and over to Pasco, Kennewick, and Richland on the Washington side. Jimmy was satisfied that this hard man knew the territory and its people. He was satisfied, also, that Timmons was trying hard to cover all the bases to obtain maximum sales.

It struck Jimmy that if someone heard the two men talking, it would seem to them that the product that they sold was machinery and equipment for the many different industries in the area. There had been no mention of drugs, nor would it ever be mentioned. Their product, as destructive as it was, met the needs of their customers, just like any good product. The two men felt that the main difference in the product that they sold, and the product that their business cards indicated, was in the way it was merchandised. Neither man gave a thought about how the lives of their users were destroyed, as were the lives of everyone with whom the user comes in contact. They were salesmen, not social workers, they told themselves. Someone else had the responsibility to put Humpty Dumpty back together again.

The two men made the switch of their briefcases, and when they parted they shook hands and walked in opposite directions, Hank to his truck, and Jimmy to a waiting taxi to take him back to the airport where he had left his plane. Upon arrival he checked in with flight control, filed his flight plan, and went out to check his plane before taking off. He had not given a thought to Hank Timmons, or the amount of cash he had in the briefcase, since parting at the restaurant. Timmons knew any deviations from the reports, or the expected income, would be taken care of by others in due time. The corrective measures in this business were a little more stringent than a firing. The firing from a job was replaced by the firing of a pistol. A co-worker only received one chance to cheat on Jimmy. Hank understood that, and approved. He operated the same way with his people.

Jimmy was back on the ground at the Central Oregon Resort by one o'clock that afternoon. He had his plane serviced and stored for the night, and walked into the resort's restaurant for lunch by one thirty. Terry came down to the restaurant, following Jimmy's call to his room. He had relaxed around the pool for the morning, and had not eaten since breakfast. Jimmy's call did not come too soon for him, because he was hungry. He, also, had been pondering how he was going to tell Jimmy about the unfortunate demise of John Hickman, his Bend area manager. When Jimmy called him to come down and have lunch with him, Terry thought it would be a perfect time to suggest that they line up a new manager. He would suggest that Sandy Simpson from the Mountain View Resort take over the Bend area, which included the Cascade Ski Lodge and the Ponderosa Resort area. This would certainly more than double her income, and it would also give him the opportunity to come over to Bend once in a while. Maybe he could get to know her a little better as a person.

During lunch Terry pulled out the computer report he had printed out on John Hickman's printer, and handed the document to Jimmy. Jimmy glanced into Terry's eyes, and then he scanned the report. He nodded as he finished reading, and handed it back to Terry. Without an expression on his face he asked how Terry had handled it. Terry brought up the subject that they would have to replace the man. Jimmy, realizing the implication of the suggestion, asked if he had thought of a possible replacement in this lucrative area. When Terry made his suggestion that Sandy could handle this area, also, Jimmy's eyebrows went up. He was not against the suggestion, but he had not expected it from Terry.

Terry went on to show how Sandy had held down the position of supplying the needs of her clientele at Mountain View Resort with their product, and with other entertainment from her established acquaintances. She was already capable of managing people, so she could easily manage the additional people for this area. Jimmy was impressed with Terry's logic of the situation, and nodded in agreement. He told Terry to call and set up a meeting for lunch with her at a site outside of Mountain View Resort. Terry smiled at how well it had gone, and the acceptance of his plan. He would call and set up a lunch at the Crossroads Restaurant in Sisters for Saturday around noon.

That evening, Jimmy and Terry met in Jimmy's condo. They locked the door, chained it, and set a chair under the doorknob to prevent any entry through the door. They went into his master bedroom suite, which had a table and four chairs at one end. Pulling the drapes, and turning on some music, he effectively shut out any visual or auditory contact. Terry brought in a total of six identical brown leather covered metal framed briefcases that had been exchanged with the area managers they had visited. He emptied each in turn onto the table. After the contents of each had been reviewed by a thorough analysis of the reports, Jimmy entered the summary data into the laptop computer that he carried on his trips. The spreadsheet he used was compatible with the main computer in his office in Portland, and the information could be dumped into it when he got back, or it could be sent back by modem. Jimmy was never too comfortable sending the information over telephone wires, so he had never used that feature. He felt that telephone taps and possible access by others would undermine security that he required.

The piles of money that developed as it was counted and stacked was quite impressive. Jimmy and Terry really did not like handling the money, because the bills were so dirty. The bills also gave off odors of those from whom it had originated. The smell of tobacco, liquor, marijuana, and other drugs wafted up as they counted and sorted the bills. They both felt grateful for the air conditioner that moved and cleansed the air. Although neither would ever say it, the word "laundering" of drug money could be used literally, rather than symbolically. The phrase "dirty money" was true, also, in the physical sense, but it was just part of the job. It was another one of the more unpleasant parts.

The trip to central Oregon, southern Idaho, and the southern Washington Cascades had netted about five hundred thousand dollars. That was a little below the normal, but with certain corrections and training the "take" would increase. Jimmy could explain the necessity of changing personnel in this area, and Terry's ability to act when it was necessary. The cartel really did not like to get involved in unnecessary killings, but if the situation called for it, they condoned and expected it. In fact, a brutal murder had a way of keeping all personnel aware of that possibility in their relationship.

Terry's call to Sandy Simpson had thrilled her about the potential of the position, and at the same time caused some concern over where it would lead. On the one hand she could reach her financial goals much faster than she had planned. She dreamed of owning her own ranch around Sisters, stocked with horses and livestock, and a ranch house in which she could really entertain her friends. This new position would allow her to cut several years off her time line for reaching the goal that she had established on the basis of her present income. She would have enough money to attain to the social height that she desired. Her friends and family would finally recognize her abilities. Money was the medium for which everyone gauged your success in life, and it was important to be considered successful by the world's standard.

On the other hand she knew the code of the cartel. They required absolute obedience to their rules. Silence at all costs, honesty beyond reproach, dedication in work, and a lifestyle that would not bring investigations. Sandy felt she could do all that, especially for the length of time it took to obtain her goals. She had certain reservations about her ability to get out when the time came, but she would cross that bridge when she came to it. All things considered, it would be exciting to try something more challenging. She had made up her mind to meet with Terry and his boss, Jimmy, at noon for lunch at the Crossing in Sisters on Saturday.

Jimmy and Terry decided to take a booth overlooking the parking lot so they could watch for Sandy when she arrived. As they came into the restaurant they saw the couple that they had spoken to on the trail at Paulina Peak a few days earlier. It was strange that they would run into them again, but there was no reason to think that the meeting was anything more than a coincidence. Sandy was late so they could not order. They sat there nibbling on some carrot sticks that had been served upon their arrival. Terry slipped out and called the Mountain View Resort Lodge and asked if Sandy was there. The receptionist said that she had left for lunch, and she would not be back until about one thirty. Terry thanked her and said he would call her later. At least she was on her way, he reasoned.

While they were waiting, the older couple that they had met on the Paulina Peak trail came over and chatted for a few minutes. Jimmy thought they represented middle class America if anyone ever did. They were overly friendly, overly talkative, more time on their hands than they needed, and guileless to a fault. They seemed to ask the most direct questions of anyone he ever met. Perhaps they bothered him because he could not shake the feeling that they knew something about him, even if they did not show it.

He talked with them, because he did not feel he would ever see them again. When they left, he was glad that they were gone. As they pulled away from the parking lot, he noticed Sandy Simpson pulling in. Good, he thought. He would get this piece of work done, relax the rest of the day, and fly back to Portland tomorrow. He had a lot of work to wrap up. He had to deposit the money he collected, and had to call Karen. He needed some female companionship. He hoped she had missed him, and would fuss over him to show it.

7

I called the police at nine o'clock Monday morning and asked for Sergeant Hansen. He was busy and would have to call me back, so I left my number. As I hung up the receiver, I realized that now Sara and I had been sucked into Cindy's disappearance without any intentions except to return her billfold. Perhaps we could just give it to the police, and that would be the end of it. However, that did not seem to be a likely move on our part. Both of us were much too curious, and with too much imagination for our own good.

It would have been interesting to see Cindy Johnson's face, we had thought, when we handed her the billfold with the three thousand dollars still in it. That money took on an ominous meaning now, since we had found out about her disappearance. It was too much for a person to be carrying out in the mountains, but it could not have figured into her being gone. If she left on her own volition, she would need money. If she didn't leave on her own, there would have been some sign from her abductors by now. It would be interesting to hear what Sergeant Hansen had to say.

It was ten o'clock before he called us back. Sara answered the ring. He asked for me, so Sara handed me the receiver, but stayed close to hear what was being said. After a greeting, he asked what he could do for me.

"I understand that the police are looking for a missing person by the name of Cindy M. Johnson. Is that correct?" I answered, with a question.

"Yes, it is," he replied. "Do you have any information concerning her disappearance?"

"We have found a billfold with her driver's license, some pictures, cards, and money in it," I answered.

After a brief silence, he said, "Mr. Todd, I would like for you to bring it in right away. When can you do that for me?"

This time his voice was more authoritarian than before. I told him I had some errands to run, and that I would drop it off that afternoon. He said that he would be in all afternoon.

"Where do you want me to take it?" I asked.

"Police Headquarters, 1111 SW 2nd Ave, in the Justice Center," he instructed. "Just ask for me."

I told him I'd be there, and I hung up, pausing with my hand on the receiver, thinking of what all he may want to know concerning the wallet. Sara must have read my mind, because she asked me, "Do you think we should take the Paulina Peak area trail map along to pin-point where we found it?"

"Sure," I said, "and our Oregon map, also."

Sara has an intuitive mind, which is aided by her clear and logical thought processes. It always surprises me how she can cut through to the essence of a problem to offer a positive solution. Her deductive reasoning causes problems sometimes, though, especially when she leaps too fast when her knowledge is not as deep as her desire to help. However, in most cases, it has been a help to have her challenge me on the "whys" and "how comes" of solutions to a problem that I have come up with. I could tell her mind was working overtime on the mystery that had developed surrounding the disappearance of Cindy.

As we began to discuss the missing woman and to speculate on how long she had been gone, Sara said, "I believe the police should search the shelter area for a grave. If she was missing, and her billfold was in that shelter, it could have been the place where she was attacked. She might have been killed and buried right there!"

"Whoa! Hold on there!" I warned. "You are jumping to all kinds of unwarranted conclusions. We don't know if she is even hurt. All we know is that she is missing, and she has lost her billfold."

"Yes, but she would have called her roommate if she were alive," Sara said, justifying her supposition.

"Maybe," I said. "I would like to talk to her roommate again, and find if she was ever in the Paulina Peak area hiking. If she could tell us that, we could find out the time period. Then the police would be able to ask some questions about her whereabouts before and after."

Sara said, "Why don't we call her, invite her for dinner, so that we can find out more about Cindy. I really would like to know more about her, wouldn't you?"

"Yes, I would. I can't think of a good reason why she would accept a dinner invitation from us," I offered.

"I can't either right now, but after we talk to the police we will have something to share with her, maybe."

"You know, since it was a horse shelter, do you think she could have rented a horse to ride the trail up there?" I suggested.

"What a great thought!" she bubbled excitedly. "We could call the lodge and ask them if she, or anyone she was with, rented some horses last fall. They may even keep records telling us everything we need to know!" Her Agatha Christie personality was really working overtime now!

"Well, we could make a call, I guess," I said reluctantly. "It would give us something to tell Sergeant Hansen, when we go in. He might thank us for what we find out, since he is so busy.

"Where did I put that old cowboy's card concerning rental of horses?" I asked, pulling out my wallet. It was right where I had put it, with all the other cards I had accumulated. The name, Shorty Hobson, with information on horses for rent brought back the memory of our walk to the lodge the first night at the lake. I dialed the number for the lodge, and a woman answered.

"Paulina Lake Lodge," a cheery voice sang into the phone.

"Hello, my name is John. Is Shorty Dobson there, please?"

"No, not at the moment. He should be back in a few minutes. I am his wife. Is there something I can do for you?"

"Well, I am trying to find out the whereabouts of a Cindy Johnson, who was in the lake area in late September, or early October. She may have stayed at the lodge, or in a cabin. Is there any records that could confirm if she was there at that time?"

She hesitated for a moment, then said, "What is the purpose of your inquiry?"

"She was reported missing," I said, "and an article belonging to her was found in the shelter on the trail to Paulina Peak at the two mile mark."

"Oh!" she uttered. "Just a moment."

After several minutes, she came back and stated, "There was a party that stayed overnight in a cabin, and rented horses for a day ride on the weekend of September twenty-sixth. There is no Cindy Johnson listed, though."

"What was the party's name that was on the register?" I asked, pressing her for more information.

"I couldn't give out that kind of information without talking it over with Shorty," she said hesitantly. "If you will leave your name and number, I'll have him call you back when he gets here."

"My number is 842-5555. Just have him ask for John. I'll

be here most of the day. Tell him just leave word on the machine if we are out."

"Well?" Sara questioned with her eyebrows raised expectantly.

"Shorty wasn't there. His wife said she would have him call us back, and give us the names of a party that stayed at the lodge, and rented horses in late September."

Looking very thoughtful, she said, "That's going to be a real long shot if he gives us anything. I still believe it will take a search around that shelter before she is found."

"Well, that may be true, but that's the police department's responsibility. If we do anything more than inquire about her, we will be interfering in their business."

"Who else can we "inquire" to?" she asked. Her voice sounded as if she were frustrated.

"There isn't much more to go on," I agreed. "The only other person that we can contact is her roommate."

"What about that travel agent's business card, that was in her billfold? Do you think they would have anything on her?" she asked eagerly.

"Let me call the number on that card," she said, holding her hand out, looking at the billfold.

I took the card out of the billfold, and read again the name of the Agency and "Sue Rominger-Agent" printed on the card. Sara quickly punched the numbers in the phone, and asked for the agent.

"This is Sue Rominger. May I help you?" a pleasant voice asked.

Sara spoke in her most efficient voice, "We are making a private investigation into a missing person by the name of Cindy Johnson. Your card was in her billfold. Can you give us any help in our search? Perhaps she has traveled recently, using your firm?"

There was a pause, and Ms. Rominger said, "Just a moment, please. I'll check our computer and see if she has traveled with us in the past year."

There was a clicking of keys, and after a few moments she

said, "There she is!" more to herself than to Sara. "Yes, she has traveled with us. She traveled on a Mexican holiday to Mazatlan last September with another party. Her traveling companion was Ron Dickson. They were gone two weeks, returning September twenty-fifth. We keep very good records. I hope this helps you find her."

"Thank you very much. This helps us to fill in some time in her whereabouts." Sara sounded very authoritative.

"What agency did you say you were with?" Ms. Rominger asked as an afterthought.

Sara said, "Oh, I'm not with any agency. This is a personal inquiry. Thanks a lot. Bye!" And she hung up without any further to-do.

"How about that!" she yelled. "We have her boyfriend's name, and the fact she went to Mexico with him!"

Her face beamed as if she were showing off her newborn child. All those mysteries she had read late at night, after I was asleep, were beginning to pay off. They also were going to her head! Nothing could keep her off this case now. Success for Miss Marple!

"That's some great work, and cleverly done!" I said. "It clears up the mystery of who 'Ron' is in the photograph with her. Whether or not the trip to Mexico had anything to do with her disappearance will have to be determined later!"

8

The flight back from central Oregon on Sunday was routine, and Jimmy and Terry talked over plans for the following week. Jimmy landed his aircraft at Troutdale, and turned it over to maintenance for service and stowing. Jimmy called Karen from his car phone as he drove from the airport. She had been working out in the exercise room and had just come into the house. She would be ready within half an hour. Her voice was full of promises, Jimmy thought, so he played the flirting game of talking in words with double meaning. She loved it, and he was pleased that his charm could disarm her so quickly.

Jimmy drove into the small parking lot of the group of semi-detached condos, and parked his Lexus next to Terry's

BMW. Jimmy had the first half of the first duplex on the right as they drove into the parking lot. Terry had the other half of the duplex. There were three other duplex apartments spaced around the cul-de-sac. Karen owned the first unit of the second duplex. There was a swimming pool, a workout room with the latest calorie-burning equipment, a tennis court, and a putting green situated behind the condos. The complex was on a hill overlooking a golf course that Jimmy played once in a while. He did not spend a lot of time in his condo, but he had all the amenities to relax when he was at home.

Jimmy set the luggage near the steps of the condos. Terry helped carry Jimmy's luggage up the stairs to his right, to the entrance of Jimmy's apartment. Jimmy was loaded down with a suitcase containing money in one hand, and a laptop computer in the other. Terry returned to the car for Jimmy's carry-on bag with his suits. One would think he had been gone for a month instead of six days, but Jimmy felt better in a different suit every day. It allowed him to look the part he played. He thanked Terry for his help, told him Karen was coming over, and said he would see him tomorrow. Terry nodded, and Jimmy caught a glimpse of the eyebrows flickering downward in disappointment as Terry turned to leave. Terry was a good man, but Jimmy did not need him around tonight.

Karen took a long shower to soak her weary muscles, took her time in selecting her clothes, and was ready to call Jimmy when her phone rang. It was Jimmy, asking if she wanted to go out, or stay in for dinner. She told him to come over so they could discuss it. He smiled his agreement, and said he would bring a bottle of champagne for drinks before dinner. She checked herself in the mirror before he got there, and within three minutes he was at the door. Her heart leaped when she saw him standing there with the bottle in his hand, and a smile of anticipation on his face. She did not think they would ever leave her place that evening. And as they kissed, she was sure that he did not want to go out either.

Later that evening they sipped the champagne and ate the

sandwiches and finger-food that Karen had made. The food was spread out on the coffee table in front of the fireplace. They lounged against the sofa and talked, and when Jimmy mentioned his bike ride with Terry to Paulina Peak, she jumped as if someone had pricked her with a pin. Jimmy noticed it and asked her what was the matter. Karen told him of the call she had received from a person who had found Cindy's billfold, and wanted to return it to her. As Karen talked she gazed intently at Jimmy, wondering how he would take this news. She saw his eyes narrow into slits as she talked, and she knew that he had not wanted or expected that kind of news.

Jimmy's attitude changed after that, and Karen knew that any additional intimacy was out of the question for the evening. He asked who called, and Karen told him that she was so shaken that she did not catch his name, nor did she ask where it was found. Karen felt that it was a little unreasonable for Jimmy to expect her to be alert enough to get all the information he wanted to know, especially since she and Cindy were so close. The more he questioned her for details, the more she retreated into a shell. Finally, he instructed her that if the person got in contact with her again, to find out as much about them as she could. He also wanted to know all about where they had found the billfold. She said she would, but doubted if she would hear from them again. Karen tried to detract Jimmy from thinking about what she had told him, but no amount of stroking his neck, or leaning heavily on his shoulder, could salvage the evening. After half an hour of sharp questions, then an extended time of silence, Jimmy said he would see her tomorrow and went back to his condo.

Monday morning Karen called Jimmy to see if they could go out that evening, but he said he was preparing for a trip later in the week. He may call her Tuesday. Karen realized he was upset with her, and there seemed to be nothing she could do about it. She would just work a little late, and go home for a salad. She did not like the side of Jimmy that he showed when things did not go the way he liked. The only hope for snapping him out of his funky mood was if that person called again about Cindy's billfold. If they did call again, she would get all the information that Jimmy wanted, and serve it to him on a silver platter!

That evening Karen had just walked into her apartment when the phone rang. When she picked it up, there was a woman on the line who had found Cindy's wallet! She could not believe her good luck! The woman introduced herself as Sara Todd, and said that she and her husband were the ones who had found the billfold and had turned it in to the police. Sara wanted to know if they could take her out to dinner that evening, and talk about Cindy's disappearance. Everything that Karen had wanted to find out was being handed to her on a silver platter! After a discussion, she agreed to meet them at Randy's restaurant at seven o'clock, which gave her only thirty minutes to get ready. There was no time to call Jimmy and tell him of her good fortune of hearing from the couple again, which fit into her plans just fine anyway. She would have all the information he wanted by the end of dinner.

As Karen showered and changed into a sundress and jacket, she thought of her relationship with Jimmy. She really loved him, and would do anything for him. However, she did not feel that he felt the same way. They had great times together, and although he did not act the clown as she did sometimes, he did joke and play games with her. It was as if he really did not know how to relax enough to get past his reserve. He was so jealous of his time with her. He did not want to share her attention with anyone. She had her friends at work, but she and Jimmy seldom went out with them. He had become more possessive of her since the incident with Cindy and Ron. He would not talk about it, even with her. It was as if it had never happened. She had tried to forget about it, but she could not. If he remembered it, he did not show any signs that he did. Maybe the information this couple had concerning the billfold would set his mind at ease, and she hoped that it would sweeten his disposition.

When Karen thought about Cindy and Ron her chest ached from the pain of remembrance. When Cindy and she had moved into this apartment together, Karen thought she had found the big sister that she had always wanted. Cindy helped her get her job, she introduced her to people that could help her career, she took her to parties, they wore each other's clothes, they talked over their hopes and dreams, and they actually liked to be with each other.

Karen loved Cindy's views on life, and would lead her into discussions on what she wanted in a husband. Cindy would theorize that, ideally, he would be an encouragement to her in her work, and not one that resented her successes, but shared in her joy. He would be kind and gentle with her, but be able to hold his own with his competitors in life. He needed to be able to express himself well during intimate times, and during times of disagreement, also. At the time it all seemed so idealistic to Karen, but when Cindy introduced Ron to her, it became clear that she had received what she had set her mind to get in a man. They seemed to be perfect for each other.

Karen looked at the digital clock on her dresser, and saw that she had ten minutes before she was due to meet the Todds. She must compose herself, and not tell too much to them. She had been hiding her thoughts for some time concerning Cindy and Ron's disappearance, and tonight would be no different.

9

After spending four years in the military police as a desk sergeant, I felt that I had seen and heard nearly all the human complaints that could be made to the police. During my tour of duty in the Air Force, I had seen drunks, prostitutes, stabbings, fights for every reason, race riots, and traffic problems of every description. However, I was ill prepared for the scenes in a police station in today's world.

We arrived at the Portland headquarters in the Justice Center about one-fifteen P.M. We parked on the street two blocks away and walked into the imposing structure, feeling very out of place in those surroundings. As we approached the door, two policemen leading a handcuffed prisoner were also going into the building. The prisoner was the worse for wear with bruises on his face, clothes that looked like he had slept in dirt, and he had to be supported as he walked. Drugs or booze? It could have been either. The results seemed to have the same effects on the human species.

It occurred to me, looking at Sara's face as she stared at the man, that we had been shielded from the effects of drugs on the United States. We did not have the opportunity to come in contact with users and the results of what it does. We read about the drug wars, the drug killings, the drive-by gang shootings, the burglaries, the car thefts, and the rapes. We also read about the billions of dollars that we as a nation have spent to stop the drug traffic but it really does not become real until you are touched by it. The man we had just seen had been caught, and would pay for drug or alcohol abuse. The cost to him would be considerable, but it would not pay for the untold misery he had caused others. As long as there are those willing to pay, there would be a supply. Our drug enforcement agents had for years concentrated on reducing supply, but the real progress would only be made when we have a reduction of users.

There seemed to be a lot of activity in the main office with detained people being asked questions, and the answers were not always forthcoming. Some of the answers were being shouted, and the officers seemed to be very patient in their work. I was glad I did not have to do that job. The police must get their work satisfaction in knowing what they did protected the public. Most of the time the police protect the public from themselves, it would seem.

We entered and went immediately to a uniformed receptionist sitting behind a glass partition for directions.

"We are here for an appointment with Sergeant Hansen," I announced to her.

"Just one moment, please. I'll ring his office," she said, as she pushed a button on her phone.

After a few words announcing our arrival, she turned to us and said, "Go right in. He will see you now."

I thanked her, and we went into an office with his nameplate on the door. He arose to greet us, and offered his hand to Sara, and then to me. He was a tall thin fellow with big hands. His uniform fit him perfectly, and it almost sparkled from its crispness. His office was neat with his certificates of achievements framed and attached to the wall in precise order. His office reflected his personality, down to his uncluttered desk. The only item that was out of order on his desk was a file folder that he had obviously just taken out of a four drawer file.

He motioned for us to sit in his guest chairs. The chairs had walnut wooden arms, and were upholstered with blue fabric that went very well with the decor.

Here was a man that had the pull within the department to get what he wanted. The pull to get office decorations anyway.

After brief introductions and a few pleasantries he asked, "Did you bring the billfold that you have found?"

I nodded, and gave him the billfold. He made a cursory inspection of its contents. He took out a pad of forms, and listed the items, one by one, as he examined them. He did not seem phased by the thirty, one-hundred dollar bills, but did linger over the picture of Ron and Cindy on the boat.

When he had finished writing, he turned the form toward us so that we could see his handiwork.

"Does this consist of everything you found? If so, would you sign it on the bottom in agreement?"

I read the form with the data he had entered, and gave it to Sara. She read it and gave it back with a nod for me to sign. Sergeant Hansen relaxed a little and leaned back in his chair, but still upright and very much in charge.

"Now, how did you find out that Ms. Johnson was missing?" he asked in an offhanded way, so that we would not be offended.

"We looked in the phone book, and called her number. Her roommate answered, and told us that she had been missing since October. She also gave us your name to call," Sara said as a matter of fact.

"Ah, yes. Karen Samuels. She has been very helpful. Can you tell me exactly where you found the billfold?" he asked, changing the topic.

Sara pulled out the trail map of the vicinity, and marked an area approximately where the horse camp shelter was located. She pointed to it, and instructing him further said, "The road up to the top comes close to the trail right there. The horse camp is just a couple hundred yards up the trail and to the left."

"We received that map at the guard station when we got up to Paulina Lake campgrounds," I related. "Do you know where that is?"

"That's below Bend a few miles, isn't it?" he asked. "The lava flow and the terrain indicates that area."

"The Newberry National Volcanic Monument is about twenty miles south of Bend on Highway 97. Then left on Highway 21 for fourteen miles east," Sara offered, and her efficient presentation of the facts showed that she was in her element.

It also impressed Sergeant Hansen, and it seemed to disarm him somewhat. He began to study the maps a little closer. Finally, he said, "Would you two like to make a statement concerning where you found the billfold, the shelter, and the surrounding area? It would help us when we need it for reference."

We said that we would, and after a few more questions about our hike and camping experience, he gave us a pad of forms to write up our statement. I wrote for about fifteen minutes, while Sara recapped what we did, when we did it, and where it happened. I threw in our supposition that the reason for the billfold's position away from the woodpile, could have been that it had been on the pile and fell off when the log rolled free. Somehow I thought that this information was pertinent, but didn't know why.

He read our statement, and said he would be in contact with us, if he needed anymore information. We shook hands again, and we went out the front door. A sense of relief came over me.

"I am glad to get out of there. Do you feel that way?" I asked Sara.

"Yes, I am!" she said. "But do you know what? We forgot

to tell him what we found from the travel agency."

"I think we had better let him do his job," I retorted. "The police will find out what happened to her, somehow."

It had been fun at first trying to unravel the mystery of the found billfold with all the money, but I was beginning to feel uneasy about its owner's whereabouts. Perhaps Sara's scenario was close to the truth. Maybe Cindy had met with foul play. And the deeper we dug, the closer we got to the perpetrator. It may be getting more dangerous for us, too. We hadn't been very smart by not keeping out of the police's business.

"Are we going to call the roommate tonight, and ask her out to dinner?" Sara asked.

"We might as well. She probably started worrying through Cindy's disappearance all over again, after our call. We could tell her about where we found the billfold, and what we have done since," I answered.

About six-thirty that evening, Sara called Cindy's roommate. She answered right away. Sara introduced herself, and then offered an explanation for the call, "My husband and I turned in the billfold as you suggested, and made out statements to Sergeant Hansen. We wanted to call you, and talk about Cindy's disappearance."

Karen said, "Thank you for your concern. I haven't heard anything since she disappeared last September."

Sara asked, "Would you like to go out to dinner with us and talk about it? We were going out to Randy's in Parkrose for dinner, anyway, and we would really enjoy having you join us."

Cindy's roommate said, "I really don't know you except your name."

"That would give us both a chance to get to know each other," Sara argued gently. "We are in the telephone book, and have lived in the same house for over thirty years. We don't even know your name, but your voice tells me you have concern for your friend. If you would like to talk about her, we would appreciate your company."

She immediately said, "Okay, I'll meet you there about seven o'clock. My name is Karen Samuels. Just look for a tall blonde. How will I recognize you?"

"We won't be hard to recognize," Sara smiled. "Just look for a middle-aged couple who seems to be looking for someone!"

She agreed and hung up.

Sara turned to me and said, "Well, I hope you are hungry again. She just agreed to meet us."

I came back with, "I'll have to force myself after that supper."

Sara smiled and said, "You never seem to have much trouble forcing yourself to eat." Which only showed, again, how well she knew me.

Karen Samuels was a tall slender blonde, whose hair had been professionally done recently. She had a beautiful light complexion, and very white teeth that lit up her face when she smiled. Her sculptured features and her well-proportioned body reminded me of models that strut across the television screen in beauty-product commercials. She wore a chic flowered print sundress with a white, short-sleeved cotton jacket. It all emphasized her figure, and made the statement she wanted.

She recognized us as we sat waiting near the entrance of the waiting area. She came up and said, "Hello." We recognized her voice as she spoke.

I smiled, and tried to break the ice by saying, "I hope you didn't have any problem picking us out from all these people."

My nervous laugh emphasized my joke, as there was only one other couple in the waiting room, and they were quite a bit younger.

"I had a real struggle in recognizing you!" she said smiling.

She seemed relaxed and friendly, as we introduced each other. We were immediately seated in a booth toward the rear of the restaurant. Since the noise level was subdued by the decor, we could talk without having to shout at each other. I appreciated this fact, because though Karen always talked very distinctly, she also talked very softly.

As the dinner progressed, we shared all that we knew about the finding of the billfold and its contents. Sara related the story, but did not mention the three thousand dollars until the last. As she finished I was looking to see if there was a flicker in her eyes over the amount. I wasn't disappointed when she raised her eyebrows in surprise.

"I am surprised at her having that much money in her billfold. She just got back from Mexico with her boyfriend, Ron. Having that much cash with her doesn't make much sense. Where you found it makes even less sense! Did you find anything else?" she asked.

"What do you mean?" I asked. "Was she with him when she disappeared, you think?"

"Oh, yes!" she breathed. "They are both missing, and haven't been seen since the day I left them off at his apartment. I had just picked them up at the airport, and dropped them off at his place. That was on September twenty-fifth last year!"

This revelation shocked both of us. It was something that neither of us had considered as a possibility. The hurt look on Karen's face revealed that it was not only a possibility, but a painful reality. She went on to tell us that Cindy and Ron had related to her how much fun they had on their vacation in Mazatlan. Their tans looked deep and dark, and although they excitedly told of their trip, they seemed very relaxed. They certainly did not seem worried about the future.

"How long had they been going together?" I asked.

"They met at a Christmas party the year before last," she answered. "She was so taken with him! He is so handsome with his fair complexion, white teeth, and muscles that showed he worked out a lot. He can talk about any subject. I think he swept her off her feet the first night."

She continued, "He graduated from Oregon State with a B.A. degree, and took a position right out of college with Conner International, the big conglomerate, in their foreign sales force. He spent two years in South America, before moving back to Portland. He became their inside sales manager when he returned. He really makes big bucks, and lives a great life. He takes her only to the best places. They are going to get married—were going to get married—last fall..." Her voice trailed off, and her eyes misted over, full of tears.

I hurriedly changed the subject.

"What does Cindy do for a living?"

After clearing her throat, and dabbing her eyes with her handkerchief, she said, "Cindy works for an engineering firm that specializes in environmental control. They design devices that are used in filtering water, and other liquids, after a spill in the oceans or rivers that could endanger the environment. She is the assistant to the president, and makes very good money, also. When the president is out of town, she practically runs the place. I've been asked by Mr. Wicker every few days since she has been gone, if there has been any word from Cindy. The poor man is working with a temporary right now, not wanting to fill the position until he hears something from Cindy."

"How long have you two been roommates?" Sara asked.

"About three years," she replied. "I came to Portland from Indianapolis, Indiana, and went to work at Wicker Environment Controls. She has helped me from the first day we met. If it were not for her influence, I would not be the head of the Human Resources Department there. I miss her terribly. Our long talks at home after work, our jogging together, and shopping sprees..." her voice trailed off in remembrance.

I wanted her to keep talking, so I asked, "Karen, did Cindy ever mention going horseback riding with Ron in the mountains?"

I had been wondering why a couple who just got back from Mexico would want to go to the Paulina Lake area to ride horses, if, indeed, they had been there.

She shook her head, and said, "They both loved the outdoors, but I don't remember either of them mentioning riding horses. Why do you ask?"

"Oh, no reason." I said. "With all their money, I thought

they might spend time at the Central Oregon Resort, the Mountain View Resort, the Cascade Ski Resort, or one of those places."

Sara quickly asked another question. "When you left them off at Ron's place, did Cindy mention that she was going someplace else before she came back to the apartment?"

"No, she didn't. The police asked me that. She said that she was going to get some things she had packed in Ron's bags. Things she had bought in Mexico. Ron would drive her home later."

"It sounds like someone was waiting for them to show up, and they changed their plans for some reason, doesn't it?" I hypothesized. "Have the police checked out Ron's apartment, or with his neighbors for any leads?"

Karen looked toward me, and in a tired voice said, "The police have questioned everyone who knew either of them, and followed up every lead. It is almost as if a big hole opened up and swallowed them."

I thought to myself that she may be closer to the truth than she realized. We continued to talk, and though I did not eat with much gusto, we finally finished our meal. I found myself liking this straight-talking young woman, and felt she had shared all that she could with us. I noticed from the very first she tried to talk of her missing friends in the present tense. She was still hoping that they would eventually show up alive.

10

Karen drove out of the restaurant's parking lot feeling elated at all that she had learned from John and Sara. She began to enumerate in her mind the things she could tell Jimmy. There were the Todds' name and address, where they found the billfold, the amount of money in it that they had handed it over to the police, and they did not suspect anyone in Ron and Cindy's disappearance. All that information should relieve Jimmy's mind over their finding of the billfold. She felt good about the fact that she had pulled off a pretty good job of acting. Both of those people were fooled about how much I knew. They even promised to tell me if they found out anything more. Jimmy would be pleased.

She pulled into the apartment complex, and glanced up to

see if Jimmy's light was on in his condo. Sure enough, he was there. She parked her car, and rushed into her apartment and dialed Jimmy's number before she even removed her jacket. He answered in his even, husky voice that she loved to hear, and she flushed just thinking of him. She asked if he could come over, so that she could tell him what she had learned about the people who had found Cindy's billfold.

Jimmy could hear the excitement in Karen's voice, and he told her he could come over for just a few minutes. He had something to tell her, also. As he hung up the phone, he thought about his not having stayed too long with her last night, after she told him about the finding of the billfold. He would not be able to spend too much time with her tonight, either, because his father wanted him to fly down to Los Angeles with the cash he had collected. He would have to stay a couple days for a meeting with the cartel boss, Manuel Parriggo. He would catch a flight out in the morning, and be back by Saturday. His being gone so long would not sit well with Karen, but she should be used to his traveling by now.

When Karen opened the door for him, he could see the light dancing in her eyes. She bounced around like a kid on a pogo stick. She kissed him hard, and then she backed away so she could see his face when she told him the news she had. She began relating her story, even as she led him over to the sofa to sit down. She told him about the call she had received as she walked in from work this evening, and the invitation from the Todds, who had found Cindy's billfold. She related the evening's revelations, and as she finished up she looked at him intently to see his reactions. He smiled and asked her if the police had talked to her today. She said that they had not. He said that they probably would, because the Todds had no doubt told them that they had called her about the billfold first thing. She did not like his changing the direction of the conversation. He had not even told her that she had done well. She asked him if the information that she had given him was what he wanted. He said that it was enough for now. If she heard anything from the police to be sure and tell him. He then proceeded to tell her that he was going to be gone until Saturday, and they would go out when he got back.

The anticipated evening with Jimmy had turned to nothing in a hurry. Karen felt like someone had hit her in the stomach. As he moved from the sofa to the door, she felt cheated again. She fairly flung herself into his arms, and gave him a passionate kiss. He looked at her and told her to hold that thought until Saturday. He said good night and walked out.

Jimmy called Terry to come over. Terry tapped on his door in less than three minutes. The questioning look on his face as he walked in told Jimmy he had not expected anymore discussion that night. Jimmy waved him over to a chair and asked if he wanted a glass of orange juice. Terry declined, so Jimmy poured himself one, and sat on the sofa facing Terry. He told Terry he needed him to scare an older couple who had been causing some problems for him. Terry's knotted brow indicated that he did not like roughing up old people. It just was not his style, so he asked Jimmy what their problem seemed to be. Jimmy told him it had to do with the disappearance of Cindy and Ron, and they had talked to the police. The police would be hassling Karen with a lot of unnecessary questions again. Terry asked how rough did he want him to be with the old couple. Jimmy said it would not take anymore than a warning, such as an obvious messing with their property. He could damage their car in some way. Terry said he would take care of it, and he asked for the address. Jimmy grabbed the phone book, found the address, and gave him a note with their location. Jimmy told him to make it late at night, since most older people went to bed early. Terry nodded and said he would see him in the morning.

The next morning Terry took Jimmy to the airport at six-thirty for a seven-twenty flight to L.A. The unloading area for the departures was something to behold. Three lines of traffic were trying to merge to obtain a position at the curb for unloading, and the public address system was blaring out the message that the driver must stay at the wheel to expedite the unloading process. It only added to the confusion of the policeman's whistle, as he directed the traffic, and the blaring of the horns of irate drivers. Terry helped Jimmy with the luggage to the curb, said he would report to him tomorrow on the daily events. They shook hands, and Terry maneuvered the car out into the lanes of traffic to head back to his apartment. His successful manipulations were a credit to his courage and patience, he thought to himself, as he finally got out of there without damage to body or soul. The car's body, and his soul.

During the daylight hours on Tuesday, Terry made a drive by the address of the couple Jimmy wanted him to scare off from talking to the police. There was an inexpensive Toyota sedan at the curb, and an older Pontiac sedan in the driveway. A sturdy old fashioned house, with storm windows and doors, that offered some discouragement from his entry. His best bet would be to do something to the car at the curb. He could do obvious damage to it, and then maybe leave a note. Perhaps he could park around the corner, walk a couple hundred feet, crawl under the car, and snip a brake line in two pieces. He could walk back to his car, and drive away with minimum exposure. A good plan, he thought. He would make another reconnoiter that evening to see if the parking was the same, and check out the lighting. It seemed like a breeze to him.

That evening he made his inspection trip of the area. This time he parked at the curb at a city park a couple of blocks away, and walked by the two-story brown house, and noticed the bright security light mounted at the peak of the house. The light illuminated the whole neighborhood at that end of the street. He did not think that would be a big problem. As he walked around the block, he made a note of where the dog barking was coming from, and which house had lights on the inside. That would indicate people who stayed up late. He would make one more trip by the house at around one-thirty that night, and assure himself of minimum activity in the neighborhood. He would do the job the following night about that same time.

Terry spent Wednesday lounging around the pool. He always felt at loose ends when Jimmy traveled without him. He had worked out in the weight room, rode the stationary bike for twenty minutes, and spent time in the steam room. After a shower, he bought a diet drink and went out to the pool. He had just settled into a book he was reading, when that pretty, petite, dark-haired, airline hostess that he had admired for several months, came walking into the pool area. She was wearing a bathing suit that showed everything that his hungry eyes could stand, and balanced her book, lotion, a drink, and a towel as she looked around for her lounging spot. Terry asked if he could help her drag a pool lounge over for her. She agreed to allow him the obvious pleasure of showing off his muscles, flexing for her, and asked him to spot it not too far away from his.

She introduced herself as Emma Lansing, who lived in unit number ten. He introduced himself, and indicated his apartment as number two. They talked for quite a while, about everything from the Portland weather to her job with Delta Airlines. She found him to be a little shy at first, but with an aggressive attitude toward life as he became more at ease. His request to take her to dinner that evening was no surprise, and she agreed for a six-thirty date, but would have to be in early. She was flying out on a run to Atlanta the next day. He agreed, and felt the flush of his body in anticipation. They could be back in his apartment by eight-thirty, easily.

Just before noon, Terry took a call on his portable phone. It was Jimmy calling from Los Angeles. He wanted to know if he had taken care of the matter they had discussed Monday night. He walked around the pool away from where Emma could hear his report, and talked to Jimmy for a few minutes. Finally, he ended the conversation, and walked back to his lounge. He told Emma that he had to leave, but he would see her that evening when he picked her up at six-thirty. She smiled, and said she looked forward to the evening.

Terry forced himself to walk away very calmly. He was seething inside. Jimmy had not liked the delay in the project he had given Terry to do. Terry had been too cautious in his approach, and he should have taken care of it while he was there Tuesday night. Terry felt Jimmy was not letting him handle it, which indicated to him that Jimmy did not trust him. It was not like Jimmy to talk like that to him. He wondered what was bothering Jimmy, but there could not be anything wrong that would justify questioning his judgment on such a small deal.

In the conference with the cartel's representative, it was clear that although Jimmy had done well in opening up the Northwest for more sales, the cartel was unhappy. They wanted a higher take on each sale, because of the cost of bringing the product into the country. In the past six months the U.S. government had severely reduced the access routes of supplies from coming across the border. Couriers carrying drugs had been stopped at the border, truck shipments had been intercepted and seized, and there had been two ships caught bringing cocaine in southern Oregon's deep water port. There also had been a discovery of a series of tunnels underneath the border that the cartel had undertaken to construct. They were to be used to route goods from warehouses in Mexico across the border into nearby storage areas. These tunnels were to replace routes that had been shut down. The loss of product movement was very high, and the overhead had jumped considerably. The reduction in product would mean a redistribution of available quantities to all the area managers. Jimmy would receive a third less product, but the sales volume would have to stay the same or increase.

Jimmy felt that he had great success in the Northwest, and to cut supplies now would alienate all of his people. Manuel Parriggo understood his position, but that was the way it had to be until things cooled down. Maybe the change in the administrations in Washington, with the announced cuts in budgets, would reduce the interdiction of the supplies. In the meantime they were looking for other avenues of delivery. One proposed route was by plane into a less populated area in northern California or southern Oregon, then truck the product to transfer points. This might be altered by direct transfer to an airplane in case of the Portland area supply. Transferring from a private plane might be less likely to be intercepted than from a truck. Jimmy might consider the possibility of flying some product in from a southern Oregon airfield himself. That would improve the cost to him by elimination of some shipment charges, and it could improve available supply. Jimmy was open to that discussion, and said he would think about it in more detail.

It was during this time in the negotiations that Jimmy had talked to Terry. He had released some of his frustrations onto Terry, when Terry had told him about the cautious approach to taking care of the problem of scaring off the Todds. Jimmy would smooth Terry's feathers when he got back to Portland.

11

On the way home from the restaurant Sara and I reviewed our meeting with Karen. We both agreed she makes a good friend, being very positive, strong, and caring. Cindy may never know how much she cared for her, though.

As we walked into the house at about 9:00 P.M., we glanced at the answering machine, and its light was blinking its message.

"I wonder who that is from," Sara questioned, as she pushed the play button. Shorty Hobson's voice left his phone number and the time that he called. He had some information for us, if we could call him back.

Sara turned to me with raised eyebrows and said, "Do you think it is too late to call tonight?"

"I don't think so. Let's find out what the information is that he wants to share." I pushed the play button again to copy down his phone number.

I dialed the number, and he answered on the second ring. I told him who I was, and that I had met him one evening on our walk. I hoped that I wasn't calling too late to find out the information he had for us.

He spoke with his deep, slow, western drawl and said, "We shut things down up here around the end of September, and move the horses to the ranch near Sisters. Snow flies early up here, but last September it was still pretty nice up through the end of September. There were two couples who came over from the Central Oregon Resort and stayed the evening of the twenty-sixth and twenty-seventh. They registered as Mr. and Mrs. Dickson, and Mr. and Mrs. Perez. They rented horses for a day ride on the twenty-sixth, and returned them that evening. Paid up in cash, and moved out early the next day. There was no one by the name of Cindy Johnson, though, unless one of the women used a "Mrs.," when she wasn't. That happens sometimes, you know."

"Can you remember what they looked like, or anything that would help identify them?" I didn't want to crowd him, but we really needed to know.

"No, I can't help much," Shorty answered. "I've thought hard about it, but there has been too much water under the bridge since then."

"Well, thanks a lot for the information, Mr. Hobson. I'll give the Portland Police what you told me. I think you have helped a great deal."

"One other question, if you don't mind," I said, really pushing my luck. "The shelter up on Paulina Peak Trail is where we found her billfold. The shack was almost barren except for a wood pile. Is that typical? Do people just throw the bedroll on the floor, when there is no bunks?"

He came back with, "Those shelters are quite old, and are used by packers in the summer and sledders in the winter. Sledding is a big sport in the wintertime in the mountains.

They are supposed to stay in a designated area, but sometimes a wild bunch takes to that trail. They sometimes tear up a place for wood rather than cut any themselves. There are wild ones in every sport, I guess. That shelter used to have four bunk beds, so that you wouldn't have to sleep on the floor. Someone has torn them out for wood, looks like."

"Did something like that happen last winter?" I asked.

"No. Sure as hell didn't." You could hear in his voice the disgust for wanton destruction.

"Well, who put the woodpile in the shelter then?" I asked, completely puzzled.

"The Forest Service does that each fall about mid-September. They don't want the shelters torn completely down."

"Oh! I see. Well, thanks again for your help. If you think of anything more to help us, please let us know," I said, knowing that if he could identify the foursome that stayed with them in late September, and Cindy was one of them, we could really clear up some questions.

After hanging up the phone, I turned to Sara and said, "Ron and Cindy could have been up there after they got home. Shorty doesn't remember what the party looked like, but why don't we find out if Karen knows who the Perez's are?"

Sara looked thoughtful at me, and finally shared her thoughts, "If that couple was Ron and Cindy, I don't think they ever made it home from that ride."

"You may be right," I said. "It's looking more like September twenty-sixth or twenty-seventh is the starting date of their disappearance."

"Do you think we should tell Sergeant Hansen what we found out from Shorty Hobson? He will want to check out the information about the Dicksons staying at Paulina Lake, don't you think?" Sara asked with excitement her voice.

"Perhaps we should," I said. "If Cindy and Ron were at the lodge, that gives the police a lead to why the billfold was in the shelter. It would then place Cindy at the shelter. Since Ron was with her at the lodge, he must have been at the shelter, also. There is a good chance that the Perezes, whoever they are, were with them. That's a lot of activity in that area. If the police can check it out, and do find out that all of them were together on the twenty-sixth of September, I think they have something to go on. They could bring the Perezes in for questioning."

"Isn't this exciting?" Sara said in a voice that was almost a controlled squeal. "Isn't this like the plot of a book?"

"Yes, it is," I said. "I just hope we don't goof up a police investigation. Or worse yet, stumble on to a murder, and get involved with a killer!"

We decided we would call Sergeant Hansen the next morning, and tell him what we had learned. If he felt that the information was worth following up, then we had done our duty. I just hoped he would not feel that we were out of line calling the lodge like that. With his spit and polish appearance and attitude, he may feel that we were on his turf. And maybe we were.

Sergeant Hansen had been in contact with the F.B.I. concerning the recent report of the finding of the billfold of a missing person. Since it had been reported to them as a possible kidnapping, they had opened a file on the case. But as far as Hansen was concerned, the feds had not done a thing. Perhaps this would get some action out of them, especially since it had been found on national forest lands. He had enough work to do, but this one really intrigued him. The disappearance of a young couple on returning from a vacation to Mexico. After arriving at the airport and being picked up by a friend, they were dropped off at the fellow's apartment. There was no trace of them after that. There had been a considerable amount of checking into the couple's friend who picked them up from the airport. As far as could be determined, the woman was crushed about her friends' disappearance, and had been eager to tell them everything they needed to know. She was still under suspicion, but there was no evidence of any kind to link her to the disappearance.

With the finding of the billfold, the ball would bounce into the state police and F.B.I.'s court. Perhaps by working close to them, he could keep close enough to be in on any conclusion. He was betting on the couple's friend being the key to the solution. He did not put much importance in the fact of the billfold being found in a shelter. It was probably coincidental, and not part of the solution. He felt that the nosy older couple that found the billfold could only get in the way of the investigation. They are nosing around, though, and maybe they will come up with something. He would let things boil for a while, and maybe something would boil to the top.

In a nonrelated event the U.S. Drug Enforcement Agency had sent an inquiry by fax to the Portland F.B.I office, asking for any information concerning the whereabouts of a Jimmy Perez. He was the son of Jose Perez, a Colombian suspected drug kingpin in the Los Angeles area. The U.S. Drug Enforcement Agency had intercepted communications from the cartel's number two man, Manuel Parriggo, to Jose Perez concerning the cartel's Northwest office, operated as World Wide Sales, Inc., and supervised by Mr. Jimmy Perez. There was nothing in the files of these men except the father had moved to the U.S. many years ago, and now was president of North American World Wide Sales, headquartered in Los Angeles. The request was for any and all information concerning the business activities of World Wide Sales, and its manager, Jimmy Perez.

F.B.I. Agent Henry Connover, upon receiving the request from the Drug Enforcement Agency, had a routine check run on Jimmy Perez. The Oregon State Police responded with the information concerning how long he had been registered with the Oregon Motor Vehicle Department, his description, the make and model of the automobile he owned and licensed, and his current home address. The office of the secretary of the state of Oregon furnished documents he had signed in regards to the corporation papers filed with the state.

Agent Connover received from the Internal Revenue

Service a document showing his name as the general manager of World Wide Sales, Inc., Northwest, and the issued taxpayer identifying number for the Oregon operation, with address and telephone number listed. Tax information could be available upon request with proper authorization.

He forwarded all the information, along with info from his own files, and a report on the airplane having been registered to World Wide Sales, Inc., Northwest, to the requesting agency.

12

Terry knocked on the door of Emma Lansing's condo exactly at six-thirty P.M. He had worked out his frustration over Jimmy's telephone conversation by taking a nap that afternoon. He had not done that in a long time; never, when a job had to be done. He was always a little unsettled when he was planning a job. The surveillance, the timing, the details that had to be worked out, all contributed to a restless night's sleep. The little job he had to do that night after midnight would require staying up late, so he took a short nap, and he felt rested and at ease as he stood waiting at her door. He was ready and eager for an evening out with this great-looking woman.

Emma had always prided herself on being on time. She

had never missed a flight due to tardiness. She felt that she had developed the personal trait of being conscientious from trying to be more like her father. He was a man who loved horses, and he owned three horses which he had named according to their personality. There was an Appaloosa stallion he had named Skeeter, which was an anomaly of the word mosquito. The horse had a skittish personality, moving quickly away from any danger or loud noise, and was prone to bucking if scared. The name Skeeter seemed to fit the horse. Another horse was name Doc. He was stable, did his duty faithfully, and seemed to be a stabilizing influence on the other horses. The third horse was named Bandit. He always seemed to be getting into the other horse's food. He would take a nibble on your behind side, if you did not keep your eye on him. Her dad was dedicated to those horses, and never shirked the duty of caring for them. Emma liked to help him and knew where her father would be when the time came to feed, clean, or water the stock.

Emma answered Terry's knock, and when she opened the door, she did not fail to see the delight in his eyes. His admiring look, and the look of expectancy, pleased her. She was dressed in an off-the-shoulder, pink flowered print dress, and she carried a white sweater over her arm. She asked if he was ready to go, and he nodded and mumbled that she looked terrific. She thanked him, and they walked to his BMW. Remembering to be a gentleman, and not blow the first date with her, he opened her car door for her. He hoped that he did not look too much like a hick to her. He really wanted her to like him, because it had been a long time since he had a meaningful relationship with a woman. His work with Jimmy kept him on the move, and it was difficult to form a lasting relationship with a woman.

Terry had picked out one of Portland's finest restaurant to impress Emma, and succeeded in doing so as they looked out over the Willamette River. The passing scenery of yachts mooring out in front, and the summer evening river traffic, made the evening seem even more romantic than the special attention they were receiving as they were served. Emma carried the conversation as she talked about the cities into which her work took her. She spoke of her stewardess friends that she worked with, and that accompanied her to the interesting places in those cities. When he asked her about the man in her life, she said that her work made it almost impossible to establish a meaningful relationship with an unmarried man. Having dates in Portland, and sometimes dinners with friends in cities she frequented, was about the extent of her social life.

When she asked him about his social life, he tried to be honest and told her of his traveling that cut down on forming lasting relationships. When pressed about what he did, he told her that he sold heavy machinery and equipment to contractors. This included paving equipment, bulldozers, cranes, and any equipment that World Wide Sales, Inc. could make or buy for resale. This dictated a lot of travel throughout the Northwest. He inwardly cringed when he told her his lie. It would have been better not to have lied about what he did, because he wanted to be up front with her. This was his cover, though, and he had to stick with it for everyone's sake.

They walked along the riverfront after dinner, and their talking was nonstop until he announced it was after nine o'clock. He had promised to get her back early that evening. She smiled at the early hour, but agreed with him since she had a early flight out that dictated a five A.M. call. She said they could go back to her place for a drink, before saying good night.

She really did not want to end the evening so soon after such a great time. She would let him stay until about eleven. He, on the other hand, was thinking he would leave his place about one A.M., and be able to do the job on the Todds' car and return by one forty-five. If he took her home early, maybe her invitation would lead to a more intimate relationship, and he could stay until almost one. It was certainly harder to carry on a relationship that meant something, rather than what he was accustomed to having. The meaningless one-night stands were boring compared to what he was going through playing it straight.

He left Emma's apartment around midnight, and went to his condo feeling carefree and giddy. He could not believe the way she affected him. He certainly had never felt like smiling, when there was nothing to smile about. He could hardly focus his attention on what he had to do. He took out his tool kit, and double checked that he had a file set, a pair of strong wire cutters, and an adjustable wrench. He grabbed a drink from the refrigerator, sat down at the dinette, and forced himself to think of each step he would be taking. If anyone could see him sitting there in the trance-like position, staring at the wall, they would think his body was there, but his spirit had gone. Finally, he stirred from his concentration, and with every detail rethought, he decided to take a shower.

Afterward, he dressed in jeans and a dark, pull over, long sleeve net shirt. He looked at himself in the mirror, and approved of the way the garb looked. He would be able to walk on dark streets without being seen. He took his small soft-sided bag with his tools, and walked out the door to his car. He was now a shadowy night figure, his steps landing as soft as a cat stalking its prey. He pulled out of his parking lot, confident and anxious to use his skills honed by years of living on the street.

He parked behind a car at the curb on Winsor Street, between 37th and 38th Ave. It was around the corner from the big two-story brown house with which he had become familiar from his drive by reconnoitering. He left his car without a sound, and paused in the shadow of a Douglas fir that cast a long dark shadow diagonally across the street. His eyes and ears became accustomed to the night with its sights and sounds. The only sound he could hear was the faraway drone of the freeway traffic, a low whine even at this time of the early morning. He became part of the night shadows as he walked slowly around the corner and approached the parked car which was parked at the curb.

He slipped under the car so quickly, that if someone had been watching they would have thought he had vanished into thin air. He found the brake line of the right rear wheel, and his fingers felt its way to the fitting on the brake drum. His fingers moved almost as if they had their own mind, as he selected a triangular shaped file from his bag. He positioned the file onto the one-quarter inch diameter copper tube, and with strong pressured strokes filed at the soft copper. He held a rag under the file to catch the copper shavings as they fell, and to absorb the first flow of fluid as it spurted from the opening. After the initial flow, the amber fluid dribbled down the inside of the wheel, and down to the concrete driveway into a small spot near the tire. It was just enough to notice, if a person knew at what and where to look. He was also proud that the place he chose to cut would be easy to see, and it would not take a rocket scientist to determine that it had been done on purpose. He slipped out from under the automobile by the same smooth flow of movement that he had gone under. Carrying his bag of tools, he walked slowly around the corner to his car. There had been no passing cars, no dog barking, and no lights turned on to interrupt his work. He was pleased that it had gone so well. He was back at his condo in twenty minutes.

Thursday morning his phone rang before he got out of bed. Jimmy was on the line from Los Angeles. He gave his report of what he had done to leave his calling card on the Todds' car, and how easily it had gone. Jimmy hesitated a moment and then told him that he was flying in that afternoon on United, and asked Terry to pick him up at one-thirty. Terry said he would be there. Jimmy asked if there had anything come up concerning World Wide Sales, Inc., and Terry said he had not received a call from the office at all Wednesday. Jimmy said he had some things to go over with him, concerning the business, and it would require the whole evening. Terry said he had no other plans, and would see him that afternoon.

13

Thursday morning I had an appointment for an interview with a large company for a position as purchasing agent. As I was entering my car to leave, I noticed a strange smell that I couldn't place in the correct memory slot. As I looked around in the car, it occurred to me what the smell was. It was brake fluid! I had recently gone for service on my brakes, so my initial reaction was to exhale a deep breath in disgust. Those mechanics had forgotten to tighten the brake fluid line, or something just as simple. I got out of the car and knelt down on one knee and looked under the car for an oil slick. Sure enough, there was one under the right rear wheel. I would not be able to drive my car to the interview. I clenched my teeth, and went back to the house and told Sara I was going to take her car. I would have to fix mine later.

She said, "Well, it's a good thing that you found the problem before you took off down Hill Street! You would have ended up in somebody's front yard, or worse."

"Yeah, I suppose you're right," I said resignedly. "I'll take a look at it when I get back."

With that, I took her car and left. My thoughts were of how little things like this could ruin your day, if you let them. I decided to concentrate on the interview I was heading for instead.

That afternoon I looked at the wheel a little closer, hoping the repair would be simple. As I inspected it, I found that the brake fuel line from the master cylinder to the rear wheel had been cut nearly in two pieces. A very deliberate act of sabotage to my brakes! I couldn't believe it! Who in the world would want to do that?

The answer came with a cold chill traveling up my back, past my hairline to the back of my head. It had to be concerning our inquiries about Cindy. This was a warning! Too obvious to be an attempt on my life, but serious enough to get my attention! Someone did not want Sara and I asking questions about Cindy and Ron's disappearance. A statement had been made by sabotaging the car while sitting at the curb! And for our own safety, we'd better listen.

But the question was, "Who could have done it?" The only people we had talked to about the missing couple was Karen Samuels, Sue Rominger from the travel agency, Shorty Hobson and his wife, and Sergeant Hansen. I could not bring myself to believe that any one of them would want to hurt us, even if they could. One thing for sure, though, it was a warning shot, and I would have to be more selective about who and what I told concerning the affair. It would be best only to tell Sergeant Hansen whatever we learned.

It took me the whole day Friday to repair the brakes. I had to replace part of the line, fill the system, and bleed out all the air from the line. I told Sara my concerns over not talking to anyone but the police about what we learned from now on. We discussed the situation in an attempt to understand who had done the damage to my car. She felt that some other person had found out that we had made inquiries; someone other than those to whom we had talked. I could not follow her logic, but we both agreed that we should take precautions, and not put ourselves in anymore jeopardy. I thought it best that we told Sergeant Hansen about what happened to our car.

I called Sergeant Hansen and related to him our thoughts about the brake line being an act of sabotage. He thought about it for a minute and said, "I don't think that your car was sabotaged for returning a billfold of a missing person. It must have been accidentally cut, somehow." He sounded so knowledgeable and confident, that I almost believed him. Almost was the key word.

"Maybe so," I said. "Have you discovered anything more about the missing couple?"

He said that they were working with the state police, and the investigation was on-going. He said that Sara and I shouldn't let it bother us anymore, that these cases can be on the books for a long time.

"You let me know if anything else happens that concerns you, and seems out of the ordinary," he said. I could tell by his voice he did not have time to be bothered anymore by our suspicions of sabotage, and would like to be shed of us.

"I will," I said, and hung up.

The following Monday morning about ten A.M. the doorbell rang. I opened the door to two men, dressed in gray suits, with conservative ties, both of them about six feet tall, and looking very serious.

"Hi!" I said. "What can I do for you?" I knew before I spoke that it was the police. If it looks like a duck, walks like a duck, quacks like a duck, it must be a duck.

"Mr. Todd?" The older of the two was the spokesman.

"Yes, and who are you?" I asked in a friendly voice.

He held out a leather folder that revealed the insignia of the FBI. I probably looked stupid with my jaw hanging down like that.

"My name is Agent Connover, and this is Agent Ridpath. Could we come in and ask you some questions concerning the billfold you found?"

I invited them into the living room and asked them to sit down.

Sara came in and spoke to the men. I introduced her and they smiled their hello back to her. Their demeanor spoke of authority, and they wore it well. This was a little different than my interviewing industrial salesmen in my office. It was evident they were in control.

But I was confused why the FBI was involved with missing persons' work, so when they were settled comfortably onto the sofa, I posed a question to Agent Connover.

"Why is it that the FBI is interested in missing persons?"

"We were called in by the state police, because there may be a kidnapping involved, and since it was in the national forest they thought we could push the right buttons to get some answers to questions quicker. The finding of the billfold has certainly brought some new light to bear on this case. Do you have any additional thoughts on how, or why, the billfold was in that shelter?"

I glanced at Sara and after a brief silence, I said, "We both feel that Cindy, Ron Dickson, and another couple were registered under the names of Mr. and Mrs. Perez, on the nights of September twenty-sixth and twenty-seventh at the Paulina Lake Lodge."

Both Agents narrowed their eyes, Ridpath spoke this time.

"How did you come to that conclusion, Mr. Todd?"

Sara answered for me by saying, "John called the lodge and spoke to the manager, Shorty Hobson, and to his wife. They had registration records for that period, and they also rented horses for the twenty-sixth."

She spoke very fast and you could see the questions starting to form in the eyes of the agents.

"What triggered you to make a call to the lodge?" Ridpath queried, finding it hard to connect.

I thought I had better clarify, and explained, "When we got

home from our camping trip, we looked up Cindy's phone number in the phone book and tried to call her. Her roommate answered, and when I told her about the billfold she said that Cindy was missing, she said that we should take it directly to Sergeant Hansen in Missing Persons.

We took the billfold to Sergeant Hansen on Monday. When we got home, we were discussing the fact that the billfold was found in a horse shelter, and we thought we would call the lodge and ask if Cindy and Ron had rented horses that weekend. That evening we invited her roommate out to dinner to discuss Cindy's disappearance.

"Her roommate? What is her name?" Connover interrupted to ask. He was looking for that information in a notebook in his hand.

Perturbed over his checking my statements, I said, "The Portland Police has the information, if you want to verify. Her name is Karen Samuels."

Ignoring my reference about checking with the Portland Police, Connover asked, "Did she tell you anything else about Cindy?"

"We talked to her that evening, and she told us she picked Cindy and her boyfriend up from the airport upon arrival from Mexico, where they had gone on their vacation. She had dropped them off at Ron's apartment, and he was to bring her home after she picked up some things she had packed in his suitcase."

"Yes, I see that in the report," the older agent said as he thumbed through his notes.

Sara asked if there was any significance of Cindy's billfold containing three thousand dollars, after spending two weeks on vacation?

"It may seem like a lot to have out in the woods, but she had a good job that paid well. We are checking into her financial transactions, and we may find out more as the investigation proceeds," Ridpath offered as his official pronouncement.

"We will make some inquiries at the lodge, maybe we can nail down the exact time period that the couple came and left there. This is a good piece of information that you have given us. I'd appreciate your letting us know if you think of anything else that might help," Connover said as they both rose to leave. They seemed to know what the other was going to do before it happened. They made a good team harnessed together like that.

They gave us their business cards with their telephone numbers, and went out the door. Agent Connover hesitated on the porch and looking directly at us, spoke a warning that left a chill.

"You understand that you should not interfere in any way with this investigation, don't you? We could be looking into kidnapping, murder, and the possibility of drug related activities. If you, or anyone else, gets in the way, it could be fatal for you. I don't want to scare you unduly, but just remember what I said. And please, call either of us if you think of anything more."

As they sped off in their car, the chill they left wasn't from the breeze. If the FBI was on the case, it meant more than just the murder we supposed. He had warned us about drug deals. Was that just a scare tactic? Or more likely, was he was giving us a hint of what our messing around might bring. Drug money! That may be the reason for so much cash in the billfold! These thoughts came fast, and by the look on Sara's face, she had not missed the significance of his statement either.

"Let's go for a walk," she said, almost in a whisper.

"O.K.," I said. "We need to get out of here for a while."

Over the years we had established a walking route of one mile, or two miles if we wanted to extend the time out of doors. Our walking sometimes was as automatic as breathing, and as we walked, we talked over the problems or joys of the day. The route started through the Dorset Park with all its tall Douglas fir trees that stood near the baseball diamonds and the playground area. A walking path had been installed by a volunteer group, but our walk took us through the park, and then around several blocks in the neighborhood. The circuit was complete when we climbed the steps to our house. Sometimes we had talked the entire time, and had never noticed we had completed the circuit until we arrived back home. This was one of those times. Our talk was reliving the FBI's visit, and their warning. We were glad that they were taking an interest in the case. We were also convinced that we would not get involved anymore. Maybe we could find out someday from Karen Samuels if the investigators ever found out anything about the missing couple. No more poking around by us, looking for clues.

We didn't have to look for clues anymore. When we got home that evening after going out to dinner at a nearby Chinese restaurant, there were clues everywhere in our house! Our new living room sofa was slashed, tables overturned, lamps broken, and magazines and papers scattered everywhere. Someone had broken in through the back door, and had really done a number on our house. Vandalism seems so wasteful and useless when it is someone else's property. But when it is your own, a sense of violation of your person swells up in you. You want to strike back and hit someone, or something. This was not going unpunished! Even if it was a warning, the police had to catch these guys. The safety of our home had been violated, and until they were caught we would not be safe.

I called 911 and gave a woman the information on what had happened. She said that a police patrol would be out. Since there was no one hurt, it would take a few minutes before they could respond. She was close. It took thirty minutes, which seems like hours when you are waiting for someone. Two policemen came out and made a report. They said they would have someone come out in the morning to take some pictures, and that it would be a good idea to leave everything like it was. I could put something over the broken door pane in the back door. They would have a patrol car in the area keep an eye on things for a while.

We left everything pretty much as it was, except I attached a piece of plywood over the broken pane in the door. Sara and I had talked several times about getting a more secure door for the back of the house. The door was at least fifty years old. It was quite a beautiful door for the dining room entrance from the backyard. The door was made up of five rows of three glass window panes. Each of the panes was nine inches by twelve inches separated by only one inch wooden decorative strips, very much like the windows of that period. It was very easy to break a pane close to the doorknob, reach in, unlock the knob, and walk right in. It had no dead bolt lock, no solid door or anything. The storm door offered some security, but not much. The door and most of the windows had the same window pane pattern. A pattern that looked good for the period it was constructed, but in today's world it was an invitation for anyone trying to gain entrance illegally.

    I resolved to replace that door with one that would give us a little more security as soon as I could afford it.

14

Thursday afternoon Terry Mandano picked up Jimmy Perez from the Portland airport, upon Jimmy's arrival on a United Airlines flight from Los Angeles. Terry met him as he walked up the ramp from the plane into the waiting room. Terry could see by the set of his jaw, that the meeting with the cartels, Manuel Parriggo, Jimmy's father, and others in the business, had not gone well. The two men shook hands, Terry asked about his flight just to keep the conversation light, and they walked toward the baggage claim area. Jimmy asked Terry what he had been doing with himself, other than the little job he had done for him, while he had been gone. Terry said that he had not heard from Karen, but had taken out the flight stewardess, Emma Lansing, who lived across the street, and they had a great time. Jimmy cracked a smile at the way Terry had mentioned her name, and the way he talked. He had never seen Terry so animated over a woman before. He told Terry he had better watch himself. The way Terry talked about her, he would end up a homebody with children! Jimmy almost laughed aloud when Terry blushed and mumbled that he did not think that would ever happen. Jimmy would have to meet this gal. Anyone that could soften Terry's heart, must really be something!

As they cleared the airport on the way home, Jimmy began to fill Terry in on the new arrangement with the cartel. The cost of crack cocaine was going to be higher, there would be a shortage of supply for the Northwest, and they would have to assist in the transportation into Portland. Terry did not like the sound of all this, because higher prices and shorter supplies would bring attention to robberies and thefts caused by users. The additional risk of being caught up in a crackdown on drugs from such activities was potentially serious. The risk from helping with the procurement was an even greater risk. The feds were really getting tough all over the United States. He voiced his opinion that perhaps they could cutdown some of the territory they served, and lay low for a while. Jimmy, however, related that he had suggested the same to Manuel Parriggo, but was told that the cartel would experience a severe financial cash flow problem. Without a fairly high income, their operation here in the Northwest would also suffer. The cost of the product would have to be pumped up, and they would have to adjust their sales by covering the more lucrative areas. All others would have to suffer.

Upon arrival at their condo complex, Jimmy said he would take a shower and then look at the mail. Afterward, they would get together again to plan out what sales areas to concentrate on, and which to drop.

He wanted to get things pretty well planned before Karen came from work. She would be calling soon, he knew, and would not be prevented from being with him tonight after six o'clock. Terry said he would be back at three. That would give them three hours before she would be calling. They could finish up tomorrow.

Jimmy had just stepped out of the shower when the phone rang. It was Karen, asking how his flight had gone, and when could they get together. She sounded excited and happy to have him home. He asked her if she wanted to go out, and she replied that it seemed like it had been ages since they had gone out, and it was a great idea. He said he would pick her up around seven o'clock. Terry tapped on his door a couple minutes before three o'clock. Opening the door, Jimmy smiled at Terry's promptness. Terry was always serious minded in his approach to business affairs. He had his business face on this time, and Jimmy knew he was concerned over which of the areas that would be dropped. Terry had helped build up the business in the Northwest, and he was going to make a pitch to save a much as possible. He would do what Jimmy wanted to do, but he would offer his opinion, anyway.

The two men spread the contents of their briefcases of sales and profit records on the table in front of them. They decided to make the selection on which area was dropped, and which they would keep, on the basis of cost. The cost would be weighed by a factor for growth in the future. For example, if an area had been recently established, and the prospect of future sales was expected to grow this year by an agreed on figure of twenty-five percent, it was decided to add that figure to the current sales. The cost of doing business in that area would be amortized over the larger figure, thus making the proposed profit percentage higher. The areas that had little or no sales growth to date would then be saddled with the new cost figures being used, which would show the projected profit percentage at the resulting lower figure.

As the two men figured out what they would do, it became clear that the projected higher profit percentage areas were in the areas with the highest sales, or forecasted higher sales. This would stop the flow of product to the marginal areas in the outlying districts. Jimmy cringed at the thought of the eastern Washington, Walla Walla, southern Idaho, and southeastern Oregon areas being dropped. His concentration would be the resort areas in central Oregon, the coastal resorts, the Portland-Vancouver area, and the Seattle area. The territory would be cut by a third, but sales volume would only drop fifteen percent. He would go with those figures, and throw in a factor for loss sales due to the higher prices. The total profit would be down somewhat, but the cartel would have to realize that one could only do so much. He knew that he would be hearing from Manuel Parriggo, and would have to have his figures ready to defend his proposal.

His dinner with Karen went great. The atmosphere of the nightclub was subdued, and as they danced Karen pressed her head on his chest, loving every minute of their time together. He felt that he had needed a night out to take his mind off the week's pressure. Events seemed to be pulling him, rather than he being in control. It unsettled him, somewhat, his work taking on this new demand, following the reported finding of Cindy's billfold, along with Terry's removal of the area manager in Bend, and the necessity of trying to keep those Todds from getting any more involved with the police. The events were happening too fast, unplanned, and uncontrolled. Maybe it will settle down to a routine, now that he was back and keeping a close watch on things. The evening had stirred up a great desire for Karen, and her need to cling to him suited him just fine. She seemed to have needed the evening as well.

Sunday morning Jimmy got a call from Jose Perez, his father, in Los Angeles. The cartel's security chief had received a message that the feds were looking into World Wide Sales, Inc., Northwest and Jimmy Perez's activities. The informant inside the government's Drug and Firearms Enforcement Agency who passed on the information believed the FBI was investigating him, also, in regards to a missing person's report. They had reports on his association with a girlfriend of the missing couple. The two agencies did not have anything concrete as yet, but they were like bloodhounds on a scent. He suggested that Jimmy lie low for a period. Jose Perez related all this as if he was reading the Sunday paper.

Jimmy knew it could become serious, if he ignored the warning. Perhaps he could take some time off, and go on vacation a couple of weeks to the islands. Before he left, he thought the Todds needed a real warning this time. They must not have read the signs of the cutting of the brake lining. He would give Terry that little job. This time he would do some real damage, and give them a good scare. Terry could do it tomorrow evening. He could wait for an opportunity to strike while they were out, and mess up their place, during the daylight hours! That would give them a real scare, and perhaps throw the police off the track. He could make it look like thieves and vandals. By the time he got back, if there were no more police or fed activities he would start planning what else he had to do.

Jimmy called Terry over to his place, and instructed him to vandalize the Todd's house Monday night. He should keep an eye on their place, and if they go out during the evening, get in and out in a hurry. In the last resort he should burn them out, if they do not leave. Give them a chance to get out. Terry was to scare them, not kill them. Right now they did not need another murder investigation on top of everything else.

Around seven-thirty Monday evening, Terry drove to the neighborhood, parked near Dorset Park among other cars, and strolled the neighborhood. As he passed the driveway of the two-tone brown house, he saw that one of the cars was gone. He reached into his pocket and took out a dog leash he had purchased for a decoy, and strolled up the driveway and into the backyard. He looked like a person searching for a dog that had gone astray. He made little noise, and looking around in the Todd's backyard, it was obvious that no one could see him. There was a six-feet-high laurel hedge completely around the yard. It not only prevented people from seeing in, but helped muffle the sounds coming out. He tried the back screen door, and it opened to his pull. The door was more decorative than anything else, and he easily obtained entry. He pulled out a roll of electrical tape from his pocket, placed two strips of tape, shaped like an "x," across a pane of glass, and with a sharp tap with a gloved hand broke the glass. The glass fell inwardly making very little noise, and he reached into the opening and turned the doorknob. He entered, shut the door, and silently walked through the house. No one was at home, as he had surmised, so he walked into the living room and began to ruin some very fine furniture and fixtures.

He left the same way he got in. He walked down the driveway and ahead down the street, a man looking for a nonexistent pet dog that had run away from home.

15

Sergeant Hansen and a patrolman came out to investigate the damage the next morning. He took our statements and took pictures of the damage done to our house. Coupled with the vandalism of my car's brakes, the incidents took on more serious connotations. There was no direct evidence linking the vandalism to the investigation of the missing couple, but the technical nature of the damage to my car and the amount of damage to the house took it out of the ordinary vandalism status. The timing of all this was enough for the police to consider very strongly the possibility of a link. It was interesting that if those responsible for the missing people would open themselves to investigations to the threats implied by the vandalism, they either felt very secure, or very reckless. The amount of time that had elapsed, since the couple was reported missing, worked in the favor of the abductors, so why would they risk such actions just to scare us? It may be that they thought Sara and I knew more than we did. Whatever their frame of mind, it was our frame of mind to protect ourselves from future intimidations or loss.

After talking to me for some time concerning my strong resolve to protect Sara and myself, Sergeant Hansen asked if we would like to arm ourselves with a handgun. He could arrange the training and a permit, if we decided on that course of action. He did not propose for us to do it, but if we were going to get a weapon, he wanted to have it done legally and correctly. In view of my air police training, and my many hours on the practice range with a wide range of weapons, he felt that it would not be arming a complete novice.

Sara on the other hand was dead set against having guns in the house. We had mutually agreed many years ago that we would not have guns in the house that would lure curious minds to play with them. In our opinion, raising children in a house with guns was just asking for trouble. I had agreed, and told stories to our children to impress upon them the dangers of playing with guns.

One story that I told was about an old shotgun my dad kept in the corner of his bedroom while I was growing up. As a curious eight-year-old, and while my mother was having coffee with a neighbor, I had taken it out in the backyard and was showing it to one of my friends. I showed off my knowledge; by moving the locking mechanism sideways you could break down the barrel for reloading, and the old spent shell would be ejected. I loaded a shell in the chamber and closed the barrel, showing Corky how brave I was. A small flock of birds flew over about then, and I brought the gun stock up to my shoulder and fired at them as they flew overhead. The blast from the barrel came but inches over Corky's head, nearly deafening him, and sat me down hard wondering what had happened. The realization of how close he had come to being killed, and the neighbors' reaction to the blast, were enough to send Corky scampering for home. I ran into the house to hide the evidence by returning it to its proper place.

My dad did not mete out punishment too often, because he was large and muscular and had a real fear of losing his temper and doing us bodily harm. On this day I received a spanking with a piece of kindling until it broke, and then with his hand until his fury was spent. I never touched his gun again, until I went hunting for squirrels with him as a high school junior. And I had never forgotten the lesson of playing with guns.

I paid one hundred fifty dollars for a used forty-five caliber army pistol. It was the same model that I had carried while on duty as an air policeman. When I was able to take it apart, clean it, reassemble it, pass the rapid fire target test, and listen to the instructor's words on safety precautions, I was given a test score that expedited the obtaining and approval of a handgun permit.

Although still against guns in the house, we finally agreed upon a place in the house where it could be hidden well enough that no child could find it, or reach it. Sara would only agree to keeping it in her bedroom closet on the top shelf in the back. I figured that if I ever needed it, I could reach it, but the grandchildren would never be able to reach that high, even if they knew it was there. The clip holding the rounds of ammunition for the lethal weapon was to be hidden in my sock drawer. I prayed we would never need the awful thing, but "it was better to have it and not need it, than need it and not have it." How could Sara argue against that logic? My mind could not grasp ever having to shoot to kill someone. "Thou shall not kill" had been drummed into me since childhood. I think that may be why I went into the air police, so that I could protect people, not harm them.

We sent the sofa out to be recovered and the lamps fixed, and we began to live feeling a little more secure. Sergeant Hansen had arranged a patrol car to patrol the neighborhood, and that helped us come to terms with the situation. Also, Sergeant Hansen assured us that progress was being made on tracing Cindy's and Ron's last known movements. Shorty Hobson and his wife had recalled more concerning the two couples that had stayed at the lodge. The FBI was working with them, and had found out that the couple was with the Perezes at the lake. The FBI had put out a pick-up order on the Perezes for questioning. Not much was known about them, and they were, evidently, recently acquired friends.

The description given to the state police and FBI by Shorty Hobson was that of a man in his late twenties, or early thirties, dark hair, olive complexion, very white teeth, nearly six feet tall, one hundred eighty pounds, and an athletic build. An artist sketch had gone over the fax to the different police agencies, and it would be just a matter of time before he was spotted, according to Sergeant Hansen. He said he would send us a copy of the sketch for us to look at, for possible identification.

I was sure that the police had information that they were not sharing with us, but it seemed as though he was trying to give us enough information on the progress of the investigation to alleviate our worries. His intention was to keep us informed enough, so that we would not go asking questions anymore. He really didn't have to worry about that. Never again!

I realized that the police had no description of Mrs. Perez, nor had they traced the money that was found. There was a lot of questions to be answered before the case would be solved. I could help only if I could identify the sketch of Perez. This seemed out of the question to me.

We received the artist's sketch of Perez, that Sergeant Hansen had promised us, on the following Tuesday. Generally, I can never recognize a person that sketches are supposed to depict. I look for telltale signs of the person, but never seem to be able to pick them out. Not so with this sketch. It was still a rough sketch of a face, but this time I had no problem recognizing to whom it belonged.

Sara, looking at it over my shoulder, uttered a shocked whisper, "The bicycler on the trail to Paulina Peak!"

"Yeah, and later at the Crossroads Cafe in Sisters," I said, stunned by this new revelation.

"This really creates some questions. We had better call Sergeant Hansen, and tell him where and when we have seen him. Do you think there is a mistake here?" I asked.

"I don't know," Sara said, "But we'd better call right now!"

Our call went straight through to him.

"Sergeant Hansen, here," he answered.

"Sergeant, this is John Todd. I just received the artist's sketch on Perez that you sent out."

"Uh huh," he could tell I was excited and was being very calm. "Have you ever seen this man?"

"That's why I have called," I spewed out. "Sara and I met him three different times while on our camping trip to Paulina Lake. We met him on the trail not far from where we found the billfold! He and another fellow were riding mountain bikes down the trail, while we were hiking up to the peak. We talked briefly, and then he and his friend shoved off down the trail on their bikes. We talked again when we got back to our campgrounds. They were sitting on a picnic table near the entrance to the camp. We ran into him in a restaurant in Sisters on our way back to Portland a few days later."

"This is great news," he said. "You think you could identify him, if you ever saw him again?"

"Very definitely!" I said.

"You say he was with a friend? What did he look like?"

I gave a brief description of Perez's biking friend—although I still thought of "Smiley" when I thought of Perez—and tried to recall any outstanding features to relate. I could not think of any, except he was smaller and subordinate to Perez in attitude and stature.

"Could you come down to make an artist sketch of that man? I would appreciate it, if you would. This could help blow this case wide open. If we get both sketches out, it will be just a matter of time before we get him," he said in a very confident tone of voice.

"You call us when you are ready," I said. "We are more than anxious to get this ended, too."

The next day Karen Samuels called. She had talked to the police, and excitedly related some of the same information that Sergeant Hansen had shared with us. After a few moments I asked her if they had shown her an artist's sketch of a Mr. Perez.

"Yes, they did," she said. "I never saw him before. They said that he had been with Cindy and Ron at a lake in central Oregon. It is hard for me to believe that, because I thought I knew all of their friends."

"Well, that sketch, and the information given by the lodge manager, will surely make it possible to pick up the Perezes. It seems like they were closing in on a solution to Cindy's disappearance," I said in closing.

During the phone conversation Sara took the phone and told Karen that we had received a sketch from the police also and we recognized the police sketch of Perez, and that we had met him on the trail.

"You recognized him!" she said. "That's great! Did you call the police?"

"Yes we did," Sara answered. "We also told the police of a man that was with him that day."

"Really? You two happened right in the middle of this, didn't you?"

She continued to ask the questions that surfaced as she talked, "I wonder why Perez was bike riding in the same area that he was seen with Cindy and Ron? Do you think he lives over there in central Oregon?"

After a slight pause Karen said, "Let's get together for dessert or dinner, and talk about all this. Maybe we can remember something that could help the police."

Sara turned and related Karen's interest in getting together again, and I nodded.

Sara spoke into the phone, "Why don't you come to dinner at our house this Friday evening about seven. It would be a lot less hassle for us, and it would be a lot more comfortable for talking."

"O.K. I'll bring the dessert," she said.

Sara hung up with a pleased look on her face. No one could say she was interfering, if she was having dinner in her own home!

By the time she arrived on Friday evening, I had the barbecue all ready for the salmon steaks we had pulled from the freezer. Karen had brought an ice cream mud pie that really looked delicious. It later lived up to its looks. Sara fixed up some baked potatoes, broccoli, and a salad which was one of my favorite meals. Karen seemed to enjoy it also. She never once worried about the calories, or her weight. As thin as she was, she really did not have to worry. Sara was pleased how much she put away. Home cooking. There is just nothing like it!

During the evening we began to talk about how long we had lived in Portland. Sara related that she was born and raised in Missouri, and came West to live with her sister and husband in Moses Lake, Washington, where they were living while he worked on the construction of irrigation ditches through that area. Sara and I had met while I was stationed at the air base near Moses Lake.

I told my story, also. I had been born and raised in southern Illinois. I went into the Air Force and served for four years. Sara and I met at Moses Lake before I left to go overseas, and were married after I returned. We had moved back to Illinois, but within a year or so we moved to Oregon. The love of the outdoors, four children, and a heavy mortgage kept us here.

Karen related that she had been raised in Indianapolis, Indiana, by her aunt and uncle after her parents were killed in an auto accident. She was ten years old when they were killed, and her aunt was very strict in her upbringing. She was prohibited from going out with boys until late in her high school years. She started going steady with a boy in her senior year, and they developed a few friends. She went steady until he went to a college out of state, and she stayed in Indianapolis. She attended a business school, and worked at different jobs to pay her own tuition.

Upon graduation from the business school, she went to work at Environmental Control and Devices as a secretary in the personnel department. When an opening for a better job came up in the Portland office, she moved to Portland and became friends with Cindy. They were roommates for three years, and got along well.

Her voice softened when she spoke of Cindy, and there was no doubt that she had deep feelings for her. It was noticeably different, though, when she told of Cindy meeting Ron, and falling in love with him. Her voice was more matter of fact, and her attitude changed. There was a little jealousy of Ron's attention to Cindy, and as she talked of him it became quite apparent that she did not like him.

Realizing how she sounded, she laughed self-consciously, and started talking about the places she had traveled to in Oregon. She had found out that she loved the mountains and the lakes of Oregon. She had met a fellow that had similar interests, and he has been taking her skiing, boating, horseback riding, and even surf sailing on the Columbia. Her voice had taken on an excited pitch as she told all this, and just as quickly backed away from sharing anymore, when she realized she was showing emotion.

After a tour of the house and an extended discussion by Sara about each of our children and grandchildren, Karen thanked us for a pleasant evening and said good night about ten o'clock. After she was gone, Sara said, "She seemed so lonely when she talked about her friends."

"Yes, but there is a hardness that comes through when she shares about herself. Did you feel that way?"

"Perhaps it was her upbringing by a strict aunt."

"Maybe," I said doubtfully. "Her relationship was broken up by Ron, and she resented it. She didn't care for him much, that's for sure."

Sara looked at me quizzically and asked, "Did you notice how she talked about her love of the mountains, horses, and outdoor activities? That surprised me. She didn't seem the type, did she?"

"Love leads a woman into doing things she wouldn't think herself capable of doing," I said laughingly.

Sara's question had, however, verbalized a nagging thought I had been nursing.

"She didn't tell us her new boyfriend's name, where he worked, how often they saw each other, or anything. Normally, someone doing all the things she told about would be gushing over his attributes. I wonder why she held back telling about him."

"I should have asked her about him, but I thought it would be too nosy," Sara said, nodding in agreement to my question.

"I had another thought about Karen's revelations about herself and Cindy. If she liked to ride horses in the mountains so much, why didn't she go with Ron and Cindy to central Oregon?"

Sara's eyebrows went up as her eyes went wider. "Maybe she did go! Maybe she went with her boyfriend!"

Then realizing the implications of what she just said, she stared at me in horror and almost in a whisper she said, "Maybe she was the Mrs. Perez! Oh, my heavens, do you think that's possible?"

I shook my head slowly thinking of what she just said. Could such a sincere person as Karen put on an act so convincingly about how much she cared for Cindy, and yet be involved in her disappearance?

"I don't know," I admitted. "The description of Mrs. Perez, that was registered at the lodge, wasn't given by Shorty Hobson. It would be hard to accuse Karen on what we know."

"Yes, but what if? What if Karen was Mrs. Perez? She would know everything that we know, and could pass it on to Perez. And if she knew Perez, she lied about recognizing the police sketch of him. She could be lying about picking Cindy and Ron up at the airport and then dropping them off."

"It's hard to believe, but it could be possible. If she is Mrs. Perez, that would explain the vandalizing of the house and my car. She now knows we saw Perez and his friend on the trail, and could identify both of them. Also, Shorty Hobson is in danger if she is Mrs. Perez, because he is the only one that has really seen the four together."

We were really jumping to conclusions about Karen. I wondered if the police had checked her out thoroughly. We could be in a lot of trouble, though, if she was feeding Perez everything we told her, and everything the police told her about the investigation.

All I could do is wonder. There was no proof of all of our suspicions of her. All we could do for the moment was let it lie, and watch out for ourselves.

16

On the following Monday, Sergeant Hansen called to say he would like to have us down to the police department, so that an artist could sketch Perez's bicycling friend. We could come before noon, if we were available. I said that we would be there.

To make small talk I asked him if he had been successful in locating Perez. He related that the FBI had reported that Perez had been tied to a Colombian drug cartel with connections to a Mexican drug lord. His cover was an international salesman of construction equipment with offices in Los Angeles. The company's name was World Wide Sales, Inc. It was reported to be a front for laundering drug money. He had arrived in the Portland area about a year and a half ago, and had not been seen associating with any known dealers or pushers. His sphere of operation was most likely not in Portland, but in the large resort areas of central Oregon and the Oregon coast. It was not known how he moves his supplies into the United States, or into this area. But it would just be a matter of time before they found his pipeline from Mexico.

"How about Cindy Johnson and Ron Dickson? Have you any more leads?" I asked.

"Some," he responded. "We are working with the state police and the FBI on the assumption that she was last seen with Ron, Perez, and another woman at the lodge at Paulina Lake. We have searched the area around the horse shelter looking for possible clues, but there has been too much traffic in the area. We have contracted Shorty Hobson to widen the search along the trails in and around the Paulina Peak area for possible burial sites. He knows the area better than anyone, and he likes to work alone."

Still pumping him for information I asked, "Is there any tie-in between Perez and Karen Samuels?"

He hesitated before he replied, "Why do you ask?"

"Just a hunch Sara and I have been kicking around," I answered.

"Let's put it this way," he said. "There is an on-going investigation that includes everyone who knows Cindy Johnson and Ron Dickson. Although it includes Karen Samuels, there is no definite proof of a tie-in with Perez. If you are in contact with her, I believe it would be in the best interest of the investigation that you not discuss the case with her."

The silence that resulted from his statement punctuated what he wanted to get across to me. I felt bad that I had not followed his warning before. I told him we would not discuss the case with anyone except him in the future.

We had no contact with anyone except the police artist concerning the case for over a week. We drove by Karen's apartment during the week enroute to a dining spot near there. Her white sports car was parked alongside a maroon Lexus sedan and a silver BMW two door. I thought immediately of the nine-year-old economy car that I drove. The money in those cars alone would support me in the manner I would like to become accustomed, I thought. Karen certainly had expensive tastes. A lifestyle like hers had to be maintained. I wondered, from where did the money come? Was I just envious, or was that a good question? The income per year of the people in that apartment complex was certainly far above the national average! Maybe that is why Sergeant Hansen warned us not to discuss the investigation with Karen. She might be involved deeper than we realized.

On Friday we received a call from Sergeant Hansen to report that the bodies of Cindy Johnson and Ron Dickson had been found in a lava tube hole near the top of the Obsidian Flow on Paulina Peak. We were saddened to hear the news, but we both had realized it was just a matter of time before this sad affair would come to a tragic conclusion such as this.

Shorty Hobson had found them after a couple of hikers reported their dog acting strangely. The dog was found barking into the deep hole, from which there was emitting a strong odor of decaying flesh. The hole could have been an ancient mold of a giant pine, which was made by a lava flow that uprooted the tree and engulfed it, then the burning and decaying of the wood left the large, deep, long tube. The dry cool atmosphere with a fairly constant temperature within, tended to preserve decaying flesh for an unusually long period.

The partially decomposed bodies were dragged out of the hole by grappling hooks suspended by cables from a cranking arrangement similar to an old fashioned well. The contraption had been rigged up by Shorty with materials brought in on horseback. When he brought the bodies out of the hole, a representative of the Oregon State Police Forensics Department was on hand to assure that the handling of the evidence, that was in and around the burial site and the bodies, was correctly accomplished. Although partially decomposed, the bodies would be sufficiently intact to determine approximate time and cause of death.

The autopsy later revealed they both had died of fractured skulls, caused by several blows with a blunt instrument. They had been dead for six months or longer, the exact time was almost impossible to determine because of the atmosphere of their grave. The evidence showed that they were murdered by unknown assailants, and were moved from the murder scene to the site where found. It was obvious that the murderer, or murderers, were familiar enough with the area to select a site that would ensure the nondetection of the bodies for a long period of time. The bodies had been wrapped in blankets, carted by horseback to the burial site and dumped, still partially enfolded in the blankets. The blankets were identified as being similar to those found at the Paulina Lake Lodge. The hairs removed from the blankets were identified coming from rental horses stabled, also, at the lodge.

The report certainly confirmed the possibility of Cindy and Ron being killed during the few days after arrival from Mexico, and the probability of being killed while horseback riding with the Perezes. It may be a jump to reach that conclusion without a shadow of doubt, but juries have convicted on less evidence.

On our walk through the park that evening I noticed a maroon Lexus parked at the curb not far away. There was no one in the car, and it was such a strikingly beautiful car that it was very noticeable. We ambled over toward it, and as we admired it from afar we noticed the unique license plate number, LXS1313.

I said to Sara as I gazed admiringly, "Someone is very proud of that car."

"I am glad they have it, and not us!" she retorted. "With a year's payments we could travel to England and visit Vi, Keith, Marian, and Arthur.

"True," I muttered, "but if we could afford that car we could afford to bring them here to visit us!"

The friends that Sara had referred to lived in Swindon, England. Vi and Keith Slattery were the parents of the husband of our oldest daughter. Marian and Arthur were their neighbors who lived next door to them in a semi-detached bungalow. When they came to visit their son and new daughter in America, we got to spend time with them, also. And on our subsequent trips to visit them, they treated us royally with trips around England, Scotland, Wales, and even to France. We all acted like children when we were together, and always looked forward to when we could see them again. Sara did not look on automobiles as something to get excited about. People, and her relationship with them, were the things that were uppermost in her mind.

As we walked around the newly laid sawdust jogging path in the park, we were in a philosophical discussion on what was really meaningful in life. We verbalized how we seem to have it all, friends, family, church family, children, grandchildren, and many of the blessings that others hoped to have someday. At least, we had all things that money *couldn't* buy, I told myself, only half in jest.

There was a thought that was nagging me when I looked at the car gleaming in the evening sunshine, that I had seen that car before. I shook it off as we continued our walk. I realized where I might have seen that car as we were walking into the house. It looked like the Lexus that was parked in front of Karen's apartment house. I could not find any logical reason for that car being at our park, over fifty blocks away from the apartment, so I shrugged and forgot all about it.

We walked into the house and noticed the message light on the telephone answering machine blinking. I walked over and pushed the button. The distinct voice of Karen Samuels began to speak.

"Sara, would you give me a call when you can? I just heard some very bad news about Cindy and Ron."

Sara looked at me questioning what she should do, and I pursed my lips into a straight line and nodded. She would be treading on thin ice with the police if she called Karen back.

On the other hand it would seem very obvious to Karen that we didn't want to speak to her, since she did sound upset.

"Why don't you see what she heard, but don't initiate any news about the case. Just respond to what she says and try to be comforting," I instructed her in the obvious.

Sara punched in Karen's number on the phone, and almost immediately, Karen answered. Sara identified herself and asked, "What news did you receive?"

"They have found their bodies!" she said with a husky voice. "Have the police called you?"

"Yes, Sergeant Hansen called awhile ago. I am so sorry, Karen," Sara said with a voice that was sincere. "Losing a friend that is close is hard on anyone. At least the waiting is over, now you know for sure. The waiting, and not knowing, must have been terrible for you."

There was a soothing, comforting tone in Sara's voice. It had been developed over the years helping friends and neighbors cope with the pain in living, and the void left with the dying. Sara was a good listener.

Her face registered surprise when Karen asked," Did Sergeant Hansen say anything about how or why they died?"

"No, but he did say that their bodies were found in a lava tube. They were down very deep, and the police had a hard time getting them out."

"Have they found out anymore about the fellow in the artist's sketch they are looking for?"

Sara realized Karen was trying to find out what the police knew, and had shared with us. It was hard not to tell her all the details, but Sara knew that Karen might be more involved than we knew.

She said, "No, but I'm very sure they will catch him soon."

Karen pressed Sara harder by saying, "Did the police tell you what they were doing to find him?" She was frantic about finding out more.

"The usual police procedures, I would think, wouldn't you?" Sara said, sidestepping the issue.

"I suppose," Karen said, resigned to the fact she was not

going to get anything else out of Sara. "Let me know if you hear anything else."

"O.K.," Sara replied. "Don't worry, the police will catch everyone involved in all this. And you will be able to put it behind you and go on. We'll continue to pray for you."

Karen said, "Thanks," very softly.

Sara said, "Goodbye," and hung the phone up. She turned and related to me all that was said, puzzled over Karen's anxious desire for information on the progress of the investigation. It was both our feelings that Karen was involved, and was on the edge of panicking.

17

When we drove by Karen's apartment a few days later, the Lexus sedan we had seen in our neighborhood near our park was now parked in front of Karen's apartment building. I recognized the license plate number immediately, LXS1313. I was getting paranoid about that automobile. What if it belonged to someone who was keeping an eye on our house, and the coming and going of Sara and me? The thought of someone keeping surveillance on us and our home really got to me. We have lived in the neighborhood, in the same house, for over thirty years. We love this area. We do not need this big old house now that the children are gone, but it is comfortable. It has some good points and bad, like all houses. All in all it is not too bad. It has five bedrooms and a full bath with an old fashioned tub upstairs, full dining room, living room, kitchen, utility room, full bath with shower, and a family room downstairs. The front door opens into an entry hall that leads either up the stairs, or into the living room, or the family room. We have thought about selling it and getting a smaller one, but where would we go any better? These characters that were trying to spy on us, if that was what was going on, were going to be reported. I was not going to be intimidated!

"I wonder how we could find out whose car that is, Sara?" I said as we drove by.

"Perhaps we could get Sergeant Hansen to look it up for us. If there is a tie-in to anyone involved in Cindy and Ron's murder, he would want to pass it on to the state police," she said.

"Let's call him when we get back home, and see if he would," I said.

We called him later, and he agreed to find out the owner of the automobile. He would get back to us.

He didn't call us back until the next day. He said it was registered to World Wide Sales, Inc. of Los Angeles, California. He was quite interested now, because that was Jimmy Perez's company that was used as a front for the cartel. He said he would contact the FBI and give them the information right away.

That evening we were walking through the park, when we were nearly run down by a jogger. We had been talking so intently, that we did not keep an eye out for the joggers where their path crossed the sidewalk. As we looked at him to apologize, he quickly lowered his eyes, mumbled, "Sorry," and ran on. We turned to look after him, and watched as he got into the Lexus sedan that we had seen the day before at Karen's apartment. He pulled away from the curb and sped away.

We had not seen that face since eating lunch at the Crossing in Sisters, while on our way home from our camping trip at Paulina Lake. It was Perez's cycling sidekick. The artist's sketch we had dictated looked amazingly close to the real thing. He knew that we knew him, and that fact caused a pain in my stomach, and my throat became dry almost immediately.

We looked at each other and Sara was first to verbalize our thoughts. I was glad that she spoke, because I did not feel I could.

"He knows that we recognized him," her voice was barely audible. "He'll be back!"

"I know," I managed. "Let's call Sergeant Hansen."

We nearly ran to the house to make our call. Sergeant Hansen had left at five o'clock. The desk sergeant said he would try to get the message to him that we had seen Perez's friend.

It wasn't too long before a Sergeant Krueger from homicide was on the line. He had contacted the state police and they had instructed him to check out the driver of the Lexus. He said he would handle it from now on, and that we should not worry about the jogger returning to this area. He was sending a squad car to pick him up as he spoke.

It took all evening to get our minds off the incident, but by bedtime we were emotionally drained and were ready for sleep. To help us it started to rain a summer shower. The soft patter of rain drops on the roof lulled us right to sleep.

I awakened with a sense of something wrong. It was a noise that had awakened me. As I glanced at the headboard clock, it glowed with the time of two thirty-two A.M. I noticed that it had stopped raining, because the rain gutters outside our windows had fallen silent. It was still and dark as a cave in our room without the moonlight to filter through the blinds. I lay there thinking that I should make a bathroom run, when I heard the tinkling of glass from a breaking window pane.

The sound was coming from our dining room door in the back of the house. Someone was breaking into our house, again! I became wide awake with the thought that it was Perez and his friend coming after Sara and me.

"Sara!" I whispered in a low voice.

"What? What's going on?" she mumbled sleepily.

"Be very still! There is someone downstairs! I'm going to get the gun and go down and scare them off."

"Be careful, John," she said with a trembling voice. "Don't do anything foolish!"

I was already out of the bed and reaching for the clip of bullets for the pistol I had purchased. I remembered I had put the clip in the sock drawer and the pistol on the shelf of the closet. It seemed rather foolish now that I needed them. I silently opened the drawer, found the clip, and eased the drawer closed without a sound. I opened the closet door very gently, but the hinges gave out a loud squeak. My heart was pounding, and I could feel the blood rushing through the veins in my temple. The squeaking hinge had warned the burglars downstairs, and I heard someone speak to another.

I found the pistol where I had placed it on the top shelf, and at the same time I heard running footsteps on the stairs. They were not even trying to hide their noise! I slammed the clip into the pistol, and slid the barrel back to load a round into the chamber. I heard someone enter our bedroom, and stood frozen as he flipped on the light.

I caught the sight of Perez's friend's face with his lips pulled back across his gleaming white teeth in a snarl like a mad dog. In almost slow motion, I saw him raise the pistol in his left hand and fire. As he was raising his weapon to fire, I had been standing there trembling, knowing I would have to shoot, and I had the heavy pistol pointing at the doorway. I pulled the trigger the same instant that he shot. His bullet hit me high on my left shoulder, and it knocked me against the night stand as I fell to the floor.

I heard Sara's voice as she screamed at me, but it was coming from deep within a tunnel somewhere. I shook my head and fought to clear my eyes, wondering why there was all that blood on the wall near where Perez's friend had been standing before. I must have hit him! I was too weak to try to stand, so I crawled to the doorway, and as I got closer I saw him sprawled out in the hallway at the top of the stairs. He was not moving, but I heard shouts of someone calling his name coming from the landing at the foot of the steps. Perez was asking if he was all right. As I looked at the man lying in the hall from the safety of our bedroom, and the pool of blood forming beneath him from the hole in the center of his shirt, I knew he would not be getting up by himself. He definitely wasn't all right.

I yelled at Sara to call 911 on our bedroom phone, and crawled slowly to the doorway to look down the stairs. As I gathered the courage and the strength to look around the door post, I saw Sara lifting the phone to call.

Perez was on the second step with a pistol pointed upward toward our bedroom door. I don't think he saw me at first lying on the floor. He had expected me to be standing. As I brought the forty-five around the door jam to fire, he saw the movement and fired quickly. I saw his muzzle flame as I pulled the trigger on my weapon. His bullet smacked into the doorpost above my head. My bullet knocked him spinning sideways toward the entry closet. I watched as he fell, crumbled into a heap with blood forming on his side near his belt. His pistol was still in his hand, but as he slipped into unconsciousness his hand opened up and it fell to the floor. I had expected he would fire again, so the wave of relief that came over me caused me to relax all my straining muscles. Sara came over to me while she was still talking on the phone, and I reached up for help with my right hand. I had to put the gun down before I could accept her help. I stood up with much difficulty, and when Sara saw the blood running off my finger tips of my left hand, she began to yell at the 911 operator to hurry with the ambulance. I began to feel faint, and the last thing I remember was falling toward the foot of the bed, thinking how strange it was to be able to fly without flapping my arms. Then someone turned off the light switch.

18

Sara's call to 911 set off a chain of events that could hardly be anticipated. The 911 operator had dispatched an ambulance to our house, and she also summoned a police patrol car to the same address, because of the shooting in progress. A patrol car was parked at the curb on 37th side of Dorset Park, keeping an automobile under surveillance. They were in the process of checking with the desk sergeant on the Lexus with the license number, LXS1313, they had spotted parked near the corner of Dorset Park, a hundred yards away. A woman was sitting behind the wheel, seemingly waiting on someone.

When the radio blared out a call concerning a shooting at 38th and Winsor Street, and since the house was only a couple blocks away, they responded to the 911 call. With lights flashing and sirens wailing, the patrol car pulled away from the curb en route to our address on 38th, intending to turn east on Winsor from 37th.

When the driver of the Lexus saw the patrol car coming away from the curb toward her, she panicked and pulled away from the curb also, burning rubber to escape. She turned left onto Winsor when the patrol car was almost even with her. The patrol car had no chance to swerve, since her car was across its lane in an instant. The impact pushed the Lexus into a telephone pole on the opposite corner, and the patrol car ended up hitting a tree nearby.

The patrolmen were unhurt. They pulled themselves from the vehicle, and went to help the female driver. It was apparent that she was very badly hurt. The one officer administered what aid he could, while the other called for an ambulance for her, another patrol to answer the 911 call, and a tow truck for her car. The patrol car was drivable, so after taking measurements, pictures, and making some notes, it was backed off the lawn and parked at the curb.

When the ambulance arrived that Sara had called for, I was loaded into it on a stretcher. The attendants worked over Perez and his sidekick for some time, and decided to rush them to the hospital in the second ambulance that had arrived for the female driver. She was ministered to, and was placed into the same ambulance with me. Her injuries were not as serious as first thought, and she was awake. The nearest hospital was only about five minutes away, but I heard later that Perez's friend died on the way. Perez was saved after a touch and go surgery. He would live to stand trial for the murders.

The scene was right out of television. At one time there were two ambulances, three squad cars, a tow truck, and a fire engine. I don't think the neighborhood had seen that much activity, ever! Especially, since it was three o'clock in the morning!

Sara rode to the hospital in the ambulance that I was in. She was shocked to see that the female driver involved in the accident with the police was Karen. They never spoke on the ride, and Karen averted her eyes when they carried her into the emergency room.

The next evening Sara came down to the hospital. As I was lying there with my arm in a cast, held at a weird angle by plaster and wire, she told me some of the events that had taken place. I wasn't surprised that Karen was Perez's girlfriend. Sara said that there was a police guard on Karen's hospital room, because she was being charged as an accomplice in the murder of Cindy and Ron. Perez's room was also under guard, and he was charged with the murders.

The police had questioned Sara on what had happened in the shootout, and had taken her statement. They had taken mine as soon as I awakened that afternoon. They had told Sara that I must have been living under a special star, because the chance of coming out of that alive was perhaps one in a thousand. That helped a little to stem the waves of guilt that seemed to be washing over me. On the one hand I knew we would both be dead, if I had not shot those men, but on the other hand I knew what God's word says about killing. I could only pray that He would forgive me, and that I could forgive myself.

My shoulder muscles were stitched together, and the cast was in place until everything healed. I was in the hospital almost two weeks after surgery. Rehabilitation went on for several weeks after the cast was taken off.

Sara visited me every day, and insisted I walk and do my exercises. I accused her of being a slave driver, that she loved to see my pain when I walked, and would not listen to my complaints.

The doctors and nurses praised her for her dedication, and for her attention to me, and later gave her credit for my fast recovery. I just wanted to get out of there and go home. I had to admit I was not a good patient.

While Sara was visiting me, she also called on Karen. It was through her that she learned all the facts of the case, and was able to piece it all together.

Karen had been suspected by the police of being involved from the beginning. Her association with Perez had been known for some time. Perez's first name was Jimmy. She said that they had been seeing each other for about a year. They had met at a party that she had gone to with Ron and Cindy. He was exciting, a good dancer, very good-looking, and he captivated her with his charm. He scared her sometimes with his violent acts to show off his strength, and with the unnecessary risky chances he took in whatever he was doing. She had suspected that he sold drugs, and later she found out for sure. By the time she knew, she had fallen for him and his lifestyle. The way he spent his money lured her to him like a butterfly to a flower.

The first time Perez asked her to recruit Karen and Ron as a runner of drugs from Mexico, she did not want to do it. He pressured her for some time, but she told him that she just could not get them involved. After nearly two weeks of his constant requests, and finally, demands that she at least ask them, she told him no, and if that is all she meant to him to get out. He stormed out, threatening never to see her again.

After the third day, she called him and apologized, and said that she would ask Cindy. Cindy agreed to talk to Jimmy, because she and Ron were thinking of a Mexican vacation. Jimmy made it sound so easy, and assured them that all they had to do was to carry their clothes back in luggage provided by Jimmy's contact in Mexico. For their efforts they would receive ten thousand dollars upon arrival in Portland. They agreed to do it, and Karen said Jimmy's personality changed after that, and he became like his old, charming, fun-loving self again. The four of them went out several times together, and became quite friendly. Cindy and Ron felt that bringing back the stuff would give some extra excitement to their vacation, put some money in their pockets, and have their vacation paid for in the deal as well.

Karen also cleared up for us what had happened after she picked up Cindy and Ron at the airport, when they arrived back from Mexico. She related to Sara that she had picked them up and took them directly to Ron's apartment where

Jimmy met them. He had them empty their luggage, so that he could retrieve the bags of white powder from the false bottom of each of their pieces of luggage. Ron had worried that the security checks at the airport would pick up the packages on their monitors, but apparently the thin packages looked like part of the structure of the suitcases. They both giggled and talked on the plane later how easy it was to get drugs across the border, and how easy it was to make ten thousand dollars in the process. They agreed, however, that they did not want to take the chance of getting caught again. Even the money did not change their minds, when Jimmy paid them.

For a celebration of their successful business transaction Jimmy insisted they all fly over to the Central Oregon Resort, and spend the weekend at his place. After some discussion on timing of their return, and a promise from him that he would get the couple back Sunday evening, the group flew to the resort located south of Bend.

It was from there that they had driven to the Paulina Lake area, and stayed overnight to ride horseback on the trails. Karen told of how Jimmy could manipulate through the use of his charm, and his whirlwind lifestyle. Horseback riding was just another part of it all. It was impossible to say *no* to him.

They had rolled up blankets and slickers for the outing, and tied them behind their saddles. The lodge keeper had prepared lunches, and their ride was going to be a real treat. They rode to the Obsidian Flow, and back to the horse shelter before noon. They had their lunches there at the camp, and as they sat talking about how great it was to be back, Jimmy brought up the subject of their making another trip to Mexico. He reasoned that theirs could be a very lucrative arrangement, with almost no risk. Ron tried desperately to convince him that he and Cindy were through with that, but Jimmy was like a man possessed. He was not used to being told *no*, and said that he had ways to force them to do it.

The whole thing got out of hand. A fight ensued between the two men, and Jimmy's strength got the best of Ron. After knocking Ron down, he picked up a limb of a tree, about the size of a baseball bat, and hit him in the head. He hit him again to make sure he would not get up. Cindy and Karen were screaming at the top of their lungs, which seemed to excite Jimmy all the more. He swung the limb and hit Cindy across her head just above the temple area. Cindy fell like a rag doll, blood pumping out of a deep gash. Karen said Jimmy looked at her with eyes like an animal, his lip pulled back in a snarl, and would have hit her but she yelled his name and rushed into him, clinging to him and begging him not to hurt her. He seemed to come back to sanity with her telling him that she loved him, and kissing him on his face. He dropped the limb and enveloped her in his arms, and began to shake uncontrollably.

After a short time he regained his composure, and moving very slowly he disengaged himself from Karen and walked over to Ron. He knelt down and felt for a pulse on his neck. He looked at Karen and slowly shook his head. He reached over and felt for a pulse on Cindy. Again he looked up, and with a deep sigh he walked over to the horses, untied the blankets from two of them, and wrapped the two bodies in them.

Karen said she helped him prepare the bodies, going through the motions as if in a dream. It seemed that there was nothing else she could do to help them. They loaded the bodies on the back of the horses, and tied them on like a pack on a pack mule. Karen said that, in fact, the whole scene looked like two people with pack horses going into the mountains for a long stay.

They discussed the situation and Jimmy convinced her that they could not take the bodies back to the lodge. It would, of course, be his and her death warrants. She was now as deep in the killing as he, he reasoned. Together they would dump the bodies where they would never be found. They waited until dark and rode back to the Obsidian Flow, and without speaking another word, dumped the bodies down one of the lava tubes.

They arrived back at the lodge at nearly bedtime, and Jimmy turned the horses into the stable. He paid their bill that night, and told Shorty he would leave the packs at the lodge. He took a spare blanket from each of their rooms, and added them to the bedrolls. The bedrolls were again complete, and he placed the packs and rolls on the porch of the lodge before he left the next morning. They left before sunup, and were back at the Central Oregon Resort for breakfast. They were back in Portland before lunch.

Jimmy talked all the way home, telling her that Cindy and Ron were unstable as runners, and sooner or later they would have turned him in to the police. She was able to convince herself that he was right, and that they had done what they had to do to protect themselves. They never mentioned the incident at Paulina Lake again. It was almost like it never happened, or if it did happen, it happened to someone else. She thought that by thinking this way, she could live with herself. But all through the winter, spring, and until our call concerning the discovery of Cindy's billfold, Karen said she had to take something to help her sleep.

Driving the car the night that Jimmy and Terry came to our house to shut us up and keep us from identifying them to the police, she originally did not think they intended to kill us. She had since changed her mind. It was hard to think of Jimmy as a killer, she had said, while she lay there recovering. But nearing the time she would have to go to jail, and face the charges of accessory to murder, she realized she had been living a lie. Jimmy Perez was a handsome, colorful, fun-loving, drug dealing killer, who was a boy in a man's body.

Sara asked her why Perez and his sidekick, Terry, had been riding their bikes on Paulina Peak the day we were there, but Karen said she had no idea. It may have been a triumphant return to the scene for Jimmy, or a check of the area to satisfy himself that the bodies were still secure in their deep and desolate grave. For whatever reason, it was a disastrous mistake. Not the only mistake by a long shot, but our seeing them set up their need to get rid of us.

The court ruled my shooting of the drug dealers as self-defense. I'll forgive myself someday, when the memories of that night fade to the background. I found out that it may be easier to forgive, than to forget. If Christ can forgive, perhaps I can also. I've come to realize that we have a limited understanding of events, and where we are at any one time in the human situation.

If there is anything to learn from all this, it is that we are all vulnerable to evil invading our life at anytime, anywhere, and by any method. Our only defense is the knowledge that God takes care of us, and expects us to use the talents He has given us to protect the good, and continue the battle against the evil. It takes a lot of help to survive, and a lot of faith to keep going. But most of all, we should reach out and help those who need it, because we are all walking down the same rocky road called *life*, and we never know what burdens are being carried.